Stories
and Plays

Stories
and
Plays

FLANN O'BRIEN

Hart-Davis, MacGibbon
London

Granada Publishing Limited
First published 1973 by Hart-Davis, MacGibbon Ltd
Frogmore, St Albans, Hertfordshire AL2 2NF, and
3 Upper James Street, London W1R 4BP

ISBN 0 246 10613 1
Printed in Great Britain by
Richard Clay (The Chaucer Press) Ltd
Bungay, Suffolk

Contents

Introduction

THERE WAS the Victorian who, lamenting cultural decadence, said, 'Tennyson's dead, and Browning's dead and Dickens is dead, and I'm not feeling any too well myself'. Frank O'Connor, looking in the late 1950s at the Irish literary scene, not only saw things going to the dogs, but detected a particularly notable dog grinning at the end of the road.

'O'Faolain, O'Flaherty and I,' writes O'Connor, 'wrote in the period of disillusionment which followed the Civil War, though with considerable respect for the nationalism which gave rise to it. The period immediately succeeding ours does not seem to have been a favourable one for literature. In Yeats's theatre, the great Gaelic sagas have been turned into pantomime enlivened by jazz; the sentimental political songs of my youth, like "Bold Robert Emmet" are sung by my juniors in the manner of "She was pore but she was Honest". The outstanding figure of the period is Brian O'Nolan, the brilliant columnist of the *Irish Times*. In Mr Garrity's "(American) 'anthology' (of Irish stories)" he is represented by a story on the well-known Resistance theme of the woman who, to protect her hunted men, pretends to be a prostitute. It is probably as old as history, but Mr O'Nolan must be the first writer to have treated it as farce.'

So there stands the dog O'Nolan, charged with inconsiderable respect, unsentimentality, brilliance and a bright eye for elements of farce in the legendary heroic.

Guilty as charged.

And there were many on the Dublin culture front, of his own as well as O'Connor's age group, who opined that this same dog might best be critically strung up before it could do further damage to the clay feet of revered images, or disturb the neat stockpiles of the noble platitudes and the *idées reçues*. They felt like the Scottish judge sentencing a prisoner who had spoken eloquently and lucidly from the dock: 'You're a verra clever chiel, mon; but you'd be nane the waur of a hangin'.'

The story selected by O'Connor as typical of literary mayhem and O'Nolanism is indeed an excellent example of O'Nolan's dark art. Titled *The Martyr's Crown*—and now published for the first time this side of the Irish Sea—it is certainly typical in the sense that it by no means fits any familiar literary slot or *genre*: unless, like O'Connor, one classifies it as farce. This necessitates stretching the notion of farce to include comedy, sharp characterisation, oblique satire, and strong black threads of political realism with gunfire, blood and muddle. This stretch of the notion of farce would, I should think, be perfectly all right with O'Nolan; provided, that is, that these other elements are not permitted to suffocate hilarity and the belly-laugh.

Brooding, in *A Bash in the Tunnel*, on James Joyce, he wrote: 'Humour, the handmaid of sorrow and fear creeps out endlessly in all Joyce's works. He uses the thing, in the same way as Shakespeare does but less formally, to attenuate the fear of those who have belief and who genuinely think that they will be in hell or in heaven shortly, and possibly very shortly. With laughs he palliates the sense of doom that is the heritage of the Irish Catholic. True humour needs this background urgency: Rabelais is funny, but his stuff cloys. His stuff lacks tragedy.'

'Attenuate.' 'Palliate.' 'This background urgency.' The words present for attention two qualities of conditions which affect Irish writers not, by any means, exclusively, but with rare and particular intensity. Or you could call them two aspects of the same force. Fear of imminent hell or heaven, the sense of doom in the Irish Catholic heritage, can be seen as oppressive, constrictive. Their thorny pressures demand attenuation and palliation, or else the thorns may pierce and paralyse the brain. But the pressures are not restrictive only: they provide that necessary 'background urgency'. The constriction is at the same time an impulse. The attenuation and palliation to be won by laughter is not to be translated vulgarly as 'escapism'. (Though it is true that some who look upon themselves as imprisoned inmates of Irish Catholicism do use laughter as a ladder of mere escape; escaping to nowhere.) Rather, the confining rigidities of particular beliefs impose limits similar in result to those imposed upon, say, the painter of a fresco by the size, shape and material of the available wall, or upon a writer by the syntax of the language he has to write in. These pre-conditions of work are simultaneously constraining and positively productive. Thus any literate person can make shift to scribble the Lord's Prayer legibly on a sheet of foolscap: it took a much skilled craftsman to incise it at the demand of a capricious patron, upon the head of even a rather large sized pin. The process is an example of Lenin's dictum to the effect that freedom involves recognition of necessity. Recognised and understood, the most rigid limitations can be transformed into productive conditions of achievement

You can get from the Irish Sea to the open Ocean in half a short day. Yet, development being so uneven, people living in the eastern parts of Ireland sometimes feel, driving through the west, that they have driven back half a century. Blurred, too, in many memories is the nature of the cultural atmosphere in the early Nineteen Thirties. That was when Brian O'Nolan, student, having, it was said, 'the visage of a Satanic cherub', impinged on Dublin. Some, deploring the present weather in the intellectual streets, seem to recall that the air was purer then, and more bracingly astringent, too. Others remember chiefly the frequency of heavy smog.

It can be said with certainty, and in relation to O'Nolan it is useful to bear in mind, that the beliefs he refers to in the comment on Joycean humour were more sharply, even harshly defined; were, paradoxically, both more rigid and more pervasive than they are today. They were, so to say, the determining factors of the climate, so that the unique characteristics of Irish Catholicism could be said sharply to condition the attitudes and proceedings not by any means of the orthodox only, but of questing and unruly Catholics, heretics and infidels. And this was true of all the 'pressures' just referred to.

Historical and geographical elements, of a forceful peculiarity unparalleled in Europe except, perhaps—a large perhaps—in Vienna between the wars, fused with the religious pressures to produce O'Nolan's Dublin. There are cities where a writer chooses to live because, simply, it is more convenient than the country, or easier to earn money there. The city is an hotel. And that sort of city lets a person occupy space in it, use the lifts and the porter's services so long as he can pay the rate charged and makes no disturbance in the public rooms. Other cities, Dublin notable among them, have more demanding personalities. In them, the life of the intelligentsia can more resemble life in an old-established, theatrical boarding-house, vibrant with current activity, reeking of tradition, and with ghosts of deceased denizens, famed or notorious, jostling for elbow-room at the dinner-table; skeletons in half the cupboards.

In such establishments the landlady is a character, and so are most of the inmates. Not only are they remarkable: it is impossible not to remark them. There can be no question of anonymity or indifference in the relations between them and the new boarder. Supposing that to be obnoxious to him, he may as well go, if Dublin is his boarding-house, to reside in Sligo, or London. In the new domicile the powerful personality he has fled may pursue and haunt, producing schizophrenia as he teeters between sense of escape and sense of loss.

Any artist, as it might be O'Nolan, more than normally alert, sensitive, receptive and intellectually passionate, risks to be overwhelmed by this special personality of Dublin. He may find himself drifting dismasted round and round amid the seaweed of a cultural Sargasso Sea, among what a native geographer has defined as the Dublecs. The Dublecs are a powerful, though not easily defined element: probably more powerful in O'Nolan's early days in Dublin than now. Even today you can see three or four Dublecs sitting in a bar proving that A's successful work was really written by two other people; B is a political sell-out, C a religious charlatan; D's supposed talent, properly analysed, is no more than a talent for publicity; E's reputation is based on his shameless cunning in the vulgarisation of Irish traditions for sale on the American market; the only true genius we have is that tired-looking man by himself at the table over there, who one of these days is going to write a book which will make *Ulysses* look like something for the kindergarten.

You are reminded, listening to the Dublecs, of Alfred Polgar's description of the old Café Central in Vienna:

♣ 11 ♣

'The Café Central is not a coffee-house like other coffee-houses, but rather a way of looking at life; a way of which the innermost essence consists in not looking at life.'

The problem is not simply to avoid being overlaid by that fine old sow of a city, but also to suck forcibly from her breasts the nourishment they bulge with. The recognition and mastering of these inseparably twin problems is the task, both ineluctable and inspiring, of every Dublin writer. It is also the paradigm of the wider confrontation of Ireland and the Irish writer. It can be seen as one special and vivid example of the still wider confrontation of any writer with the world: the business of expressing the general in and through the particular, the universal in and through the unique; extending the view by intensifying the vision, the dignity and indignity of man seen in the rat gnawing the throat of a baby in the tenement.

In the Irish context, failure to tackle this big business can produce either, when the Eiro-Irish takes over altogether, the sort of novel, short story, thought-fraught verbiage or observation in richly humorous vein which indubitably could have been written only in Ireland, or, at the opposite end of the spectrum the sort of stuff about which one wonders why it was written anywhere.

Most of the happenings people refer to as 'the sort of thing that could only happen in Ireland' turn out to have happened in Iowa or Wiltshire or Boulogne. They are the kind of things that keep occurring everywhere, all the time. It is a just tribute to the Irish genius, in particular to Irish writers' powers of observation, expression and dramatisation that whole tracts of general human experience are acknowledged to be specifically Irish, the Irish having acquired squatters' rights in them.

It is in this sense that O'Nolan is to be acclaimed as the kind of thing that could only happen in Ireland. He is one of those who strenuously and successfully addressed himself to the understanding and mastery of those above-mentioned twin problems of the Irish writer. In him, the Irishness of Ireland, the extremes of Dublin's Dublinicity, become simultaneously unique and immense, bursting geographical limits. The pressures of the well-known cultural heritage provide simultaneously a frame and that essential 'background urgency'. The tight casing of the hand-grenade is essential to the force of its explosion.

In this connection it is of symbolic significance as well as great factual importance that he wrote Irish as well as he wrote English. A lot of Irish writers claim, truthfully enough, that they can write Irish, meaning that they can write more or less fluently, clearly and 'correctly' in that language. Hundreds of English writers claim, with equal truth, that they can write English, meaning the same thing. But this sort of thing is not writing in the way O'Nolan understood and practised it. He had an understanding of these instruments, and a passionate love and care in his use of them which can be seen as both classical and Elizabethan. The words and the syntax, the *nuances* and sinuosities, the elusive allusiveness, the double and treble meaningfulness of phrases, the controlled flexibilities of structure, are for the writer of O'Nolan's quality indispensable matters for study and experiment. Derision, and a kind of astounded disgust were in him evoked by the products of candidates for the title of Writer who seemed to have treated such studies as Optional Subjects in their Course. He could be put forward as an argument for the theory that a writer for whom English is not his native language, or not his sole native language, is better placed than others to appreciate, genuinely master and most richly exploit the instrument. And it is true that Conrad certainly wrote better English, or wrote English better, which is not quite the same thing, than Wells or Galsworthy.

O'Nolan employed his linguistic skills on many levels and for diverse purposes. As a student at University College, Dublin, he was charged with publishing obscene matter in Old Irish in the college magazine. The magazine's Editor was called before the College President to answer to this charge. It emerged that neither the Editor nor the President could read Old Irish. Believed guilty, but thus secure from conviction, the Satanic cherub triumphed by sole virtue of his superior erudition.

Benedict Kiely calls him 'the three-headed man', referring to the man Brian O'Nolan who 'talked like a controlled and directed tempest', Flann O'Brien, novelist and short-story writer, and Myles na Gopaleen, author of that column in the *Irish Times* which both S. J. Perelman and James Thurber rated the funniest newspaper feature ever published. Niall Sheridan, friend and admirer, possibly shared with other admirers of Flann O'Brien some uneasiness about the effects of Myles na Gopaleen upon the author.

'I sometimes think,' Sheridan wrote, 'he may have paid a high price for his dazzling success in journalism . . . Did the demands of journalism syphon off piecemeal his enormous creative vitality? His column brought him vast and immediate popular fame, but the social pressures this fame engendered may well have placed an intolerable strain on his temperament which was essentially aristocratic, fastidious and private. Had Myles na Gopaleen never existed, would Flann O'Brien have given us two more masterpieces? We shall never know.'

That 'we shall never know' is certainly a sound statement of the obvious. But in my judgment there are no reasons for uneasiness concerning the influence of columnist Myles na Gopaleen on novelist Flann O'Brien. The suggestion is that the mundane *mêlée* of the newspaper column, including the literary and politico-social rough-housing it involved along the cultural and intellectual waterfront, was damaging, perhaps coarsening, for the aristocratic, fastidious and essentially private temperament of Flann O'Brien. It is neither more nor less reasonable to suggest that O'Nolan insisted that Myles take Flann on these excursions, usually hilarious, but certainly far from private, and including some toughish knockabouts. It could be that Flann needed, and positively begged, to go along with Myles. The pair of them perhaps complemented one another, perhaps were indispensable to one another's development.

However that may be, it is certainly true, as is proved by the collection published as *The Best of Myles*, that the column, though instantly topical, was at the same time well able to endure changes of time and immediate preoccupation. Its *motifs* and themes seem to tell that Flann and Myles were never very far apart. The elements of farce, elements of satire, appear recognisable in their differently shaped forms in the work of both. Very short short stories, abrupt dramatic sketches, dramatised dialogues peopled with numerous invisible characters repeatedly take the column over. Example: the series of dialogues dominated by the hideously laughable figure of The Brother, made known only by report of his doings which obliquely light up whole segments of existence, an individual grotesquely unique, monstrously typical; a mere comic figment who may yet barge heavily in through that door any minute.

On the evidence it appears that to O'Nolan almost any thesis, argument or criticism could best be expressed in terms of a story. (The use of an anecdote, an old legend, a fiction, as the most concrete and nearly foolproof way of expressing an idea could easily be described as characteristically Irish were it not equally characteristic of American and Russian conversation.) So here is O'Nolan called upon to contribute to a critical symposium on James Joyce. 'What,' he writes, 'is the position of the artist in Ireland?' An unexceptional beginning. We may settle into our seats in the lecture room to listen to some reasonably well-tried assessments, obiter dicta etc. etc., from the critic and sage. But this is not going to be our portion.

'Just after the editors had asked me,' O'Nolan proceeds, 'to try to assemble material for this issue of *Envoy*, I went into the Scotch House in Dublin to drink a bottle of stout and do some solitary thinking. Before any considerable thought had formed itself, a man—then a complete stranger —came, accompanied by his drink, and stood beside me: addressing me by name he said he was surprised to see a man like myself drinking in a pub.

'My pub radar screen showed up the word "TOUCHER". I was instantly on my guard.

' "And where do you think I should drink?" I asked. "Pay fancy prices in a hotel?"

' "Ah, no," he said. "I didn't mean that. But any time I feel like a good bash myself, I have it in the cars. What will you have?"

'I said I would have a large one, knowing that his mysterious reply would entail lengthy elucidation.

' "I needn't tell you that that crowd is a crowd of bastards," was his prefatory exegesis.

'Then he told me all.'

'All' is the jerkingly risible story, bloody funny if one may employ an understatement, which occupies the whole central part of 'Professor' O'Nolan's learned observations on the position of the artist in Ireland. (The lecture printed here under its well-chosen title *A Bash in the Tunnel.*) No lunatic attempt will be made to summarise the story. It is necessary only to explain that the narrator, the suspected Toucher, is such a one as is apt to find himself, for sufficient reasons, having a bash with a bottle of whiskey in the locked lavatory of a locked, unoccupied dining-car, out of service, and shunted into a siding.

' "Here was meself, parked in the tunnel, opening bottle after bottle in the dark, thinking the night was a very long one, stuck there, in the tunnel. I was three-quarters way into the jigs when they pulled me out of the tunnel into Kingsbridge. I was in bed for a week. Did you ever in your life hear of a greater crowd of bastards?"

' "Never."

' "That was the first and last time I ever had a bash in the tunnel."

'Surely there,' observes our Professor, 'you have the Irish artist? Sitting fully dressed, innerly locked in the toilet of a locked coach where he has no right to be, resentfully drinking somebody else's whiskey, being whisked hither and thither by anonymous shunters, keeping fastidiously the while on the outer face of his door the simple word, ENGAGED?'

One has an immediate and lively vision of our three-headed man locked there in the lavatory in the train in the tunnel, and simultaneously, as by some tremendous bound, he is outside, roaring abuse and derision at the bastard shunters, and—simultaneously again—he is there drinking a large one with the Toucher in the Scotch House, listening, writing a novel, an Irish artist paradoxically proving and disproving his own thesis at the same time.

It is not known how many people have been aware of an unpublished novel lurking in the O'Nolan archives; how many waiting to get cracking with the assessments and appraisals, among them numerous Dublecs, bureaucrats, turnip-snaggers and other victims of O'Nolanism with razors whetted for the carve-up. All may have been in some degree frustrated or foiled. For the novel was not only unpublished but unfinished. Thus the assessors must pause, at a loss to

♣ 17 ♣

know what weights and measures are appropriate, and the razor-men stand uncertain where to slash without risk of the blade folding up woundingly in their hand.

This work in progress certainly does involve the reader in a sufficiently bewildering experience. He boards the coach for a 'mystery tour', and the coach turns into a tractor which is also a dodgem car which has become hooked to the giant dipper and stops in mid-dip, the remainder of the track having been cruelly sawn away. The excursionist, looking at his ticket for information as to the nature of the trip, is not much helped: It reads: *Slattery's Sago Saga, or From Under the Ground to the Top of the Trees.*

Well then, gentlemen, could we try another approach, seeking to evaluate the matter by encapsulation, or synopsis of plot? We can certainly try. And while this attempt is in progress students are requested to refrain from whistling, cheering, tracing influences, or hearing, or indeed failing to hear echoes of previous works, etc.

So what we have, quite simply, is this young Tim Hartigan on an Irish farm who is awaiting the arrival from the United States of a Scotsman named Crawford MacPherson, a dear friend of Tim's adoptive father, an Irish *émigré* multi-millionaire oil tycoon in Texas, and Crawford arrives but is a woman, and is the formidable wife of the tycoon, and has come over to save Ireland, or rather to save the civilisation of the United States from a potentially catastrophic Irish menace resulting from the character of the Irish people and the climate of their island.

"The people of this country," she thundered, "live on potatoes which are 80 per cent water and 20 per cent starch. The potato is the lazybones' crop and when it fails people die by the million. They are starving . . . and they try to eat nettles . . . and straw . . . and bits of stick, and they still die. But a more terrible thing than that happened last century . . ."

"Heavens above", Tim cried, "what worse calamity than that could occur?"

"The one that *did* occur. They didn't all die. Over a million of those starving Irish tinkers escaped to my adopted country, the United States."

"Thank God," Tim murmured devoutly.

"Yes you can thank your God. They very nearly ruined America. They bred and multiplied and infested the whole continent, saturating it with crime, drunkenness, illegal corn liquor, bank robbery, murder, prostitution, syphilis, mob rule, crooked politics and Roman Catholic Popery ... adultery, salacious dancing, blackmail, drug peddling, pimping, organising brothels, consorting with niggers, and getting absolution for all their crimes from Roman Catholic priests."

It is her objective, unswervingly pursued, to ensure that no such catastrophe is repeated in the present century as a result of the persistent Irish practice of raising potatoes. With her limitless dollar supply, Crawford MacPherson will first buy up all the agricultural land in Ireland, and then let it back to the farmers at a peppercorn rent. The Irish Government and politicians will be pressurised by the U.S.A., in the interests of the American people, into passing a law forbidding planting or cultivation of the potato. Instead, the entire country will be put under sago: the 'one thing more productive of starch than the potato'. But 'the sago tree takes between 15 and 20 years to mature before it can yield its copious, nourishing, lovely bounty'.

In the potato-less interval before this maturity is reached, Ireland will be victualled by sago imported on the giant oil-tankers of Tim's adoptive father.

"You are a young man, Hartigan. You will probably live to see your native land covered with pathless sago forests, a glorious sight and itself a guarantee of American health, liberty and social cleanliness."

It should be just added that Tim's adviser in the situation thus arising, is his neighbour, Dr the Hon. Eustace Baggely, wealthy owner of Sarawad Castle, where he 'was in permanent residence. It would be true to add, though, that the Doctor was often away in the sense that he was in the habit of taking strange drugs prescribed by himself. Morphine, heroin and mescalin had been mentioned' but it 'was believed that the injections were a mixture of the three, plus something else'.

This extensive overture may be a third, or a quarter, or still less, or more, of what the length of the finished novel would have been. In it, a multiplicity of themes—political, social, religious and perhaps magical—are already discernible, thrusting for future development. In the completed pages one can at least see clearly the figure of O'Nolan at his strenuous and exhilarating task of fusing the fantastic with the earthy, the topical with the enduring, the particular Irishness of Ireland with the global or planetary generalities. You are at liberty to predict that the lush proliferation of those themes, the swaggering bigness of his human figures, would have overcome him at his work. Or you can confidently suppose that his genius would have mastered them all. No use asking now how it all came out. That has to remain unimaginable to all but Brian O'Nolan.

Claud Cockburn 1973

Slattery's
Sago Saga

or
From Under the Ground to the
Top of the Trees

[an unfinished novel]

1

'A BLEEDING Scotchman, by gob!'
Tim Hartigan said the words out loud as he finished the letter and half turned in his chair to look at Corny, who lifted his head sideways and seemed to roll his eyes.

Tim was wise in a Timmish way. It had perhaps not been wise to have stuffed the letter into his back pocket five days earlier and forgotten about it but that was because he was not used to getting letters and anyway he had been on his way to feed the pigs when Ulick Slattery, the postman, handed it to him. On this morning a strange enlightenment made him think of it and it was wise of him, when he pulled it out at breakfast, to examine first the stamp and postmark very carefully. Yes, it read Houston, Texas, U.S.A. It was also correct of him when he tore the letter open to look at the end of it immediately, to verify that it was from Ned Hoolihan.

Abstractedly, before reading it he had propped the letter against the handsome pewter milk jug and from the little rack of solid silver with 22-carat gold filigree (an article thought to be Florentine) he picked a slice of dry toast, generously buttered it and rammed a piece between his solid nerveless molars. He lifted his cup of blackish tea and swallowed with echoing gulps. His bland life, he suddenly feared, was about to be disturbed. Could he handle this stranger?

Tim Hartigan, left an orphan at the age of two by his widowed mother, had been adopted when he was four by the high-minded Ned Hoolihan whose cousin, Sister M. Petronilla, was Mother Abbess at the Dominican Home of the Holy Refuge at Cahirfarren. Hoolihan had taken a fancy to the little boy, and that was all about it. He was a wealthy man and brought his new prize home with his baggage to his mansion, Poguemahone Hall. And himself ever of plain habits he had sent Tim not to a college but to the local National School, with a housekeeper at the Hall to look after the boy's other needs.

Before returning to Tim that morning and his letter, it is right to add here a little more about Ned Hoolihan. His money had been mostly inherited as a result of a fortune his father had amassed from automotive and petrol-engine inventions. Indeed, it was a family tradition that Constantine Hoolihan, B.E., had been shamelessly swindled by Henry Ford I but that, through his invention of a primitive computer nourished with a diet of stock-market minutiae, the resourceful engineer from Bohoola, Mayo, had managed to get together a sum even bigger than that of which he had been deprived. His only son Ned did not follow this example of thinking out new things, machines, devices, fresh ways of mechanically alleviating the human lot: he was serious, studious, took an early interest in the countryside, God's opulent extemporising, and the great mystery of Agriculture. His doctorate at Dublin University was won on a dissertation (never published) entitled *The Stratification of Alkaline Humus*, thought to be a system of providing natural fertiliser through the deliberate cultivation of fields of weeds for the production of compost and silage, a scheme of tillage in which stray growths of wheat or leek or turnip would be a noxious intrusion.

When he bought Poguemahone Hall, a late Norman foundation of fairly good land in the west, his rôle became that of gentleman farmer and experimenter in root and cereal crops, aided by his step-son (for he called him that), Tim Hartigan. But after Ned Hoolihan had become an accomplished and scientific seedsman, he found the small farmers and peasants all about him an intractable lot. Instead of sowing 'Earthquake Wonder', a Hoolihan seed-potato of infinite sophistication and vigour, made available to them for almost nothing, they persisted in putting down bastardised poor-cropping strains which were chronically subject to scab, late blight, fusoria and dread rhizoctania canker (or black scurf). The mild, intellectual agronomist almost lost his temper with them outright. But after some years of tuberose planning and preaching to little effect, his patience finally did give out at their rejection of his miraculously healthy and bounteous seed-wheat, 'Faddiman's Fancy', for which he had received a citation and praemium from the United States Government. The peasants simply preferred seed of their own domestic procurement, regarding outbreaks of black stem rust, bunt (or stinking smut) as the quaint decisions of Almighty God.

Ned Hoolihan put his affairs in businesslike strain, appointed Tim Hartigan his steward at a decent salary, and emigrated to Texas. There he bought 7,000 acres of middling land, ploughed and fertilised most of it, and put it under Faddiman's Fancy. The rumour was (though never confirmed to Tim in a letter) that he had married about that time. When the young crop was coming up nicely, several dirty black eruptions disfigured the farmlands. Vile as this discoloration looked, it was found on closer inspection to be oil. And Farmer Hoolihan had become unbelievably wealthy.

And now Tim Hartigan was scanning the letter. If it was curt, it was the curtness of affection.

DEAR TIM — By the time you get this you will probably have a visitor, Crawford MacPherson, a dear friend of mine. Take away all the dust-sheets, protective stoves and rat poisons from my own quarters and make my place available and comfortable for Crawford. If you receive orders, obey them as coming from me.

The Lord be praised, these oil-wells of mine are making so much money that I've lost count. There are 315 derricks standing just now, and I have formed the Hoolihan Petroleum Corporation ('H.P.'). Naturally the politicians are moving in but I think I have their measure. Give my regards to Sarsfield Slattery, to the doctor and other neighbours. I enclose extra money.—*Ned Hoolihan*

Well, well. Tim sat back and thoughtfully filled his pipe. Would this damn Scotchman wear kilts, maybe play the bagpipes and demand his own sort of whiskey? But that was bogus, music-hall stuff, like Americans calling an Irishman a boiled dinner and having him wear his pipe in the ribbon of his hat. Very likely this Scot was just another globe-trotter, very well off, in search of snipe or grouse or some other stuff ... salmon, perhaps. And Sarsfield Slattery? Tim would have to show that letter to Sarsfield, a friend who occupied a position strangely very similar to his own at neighbouring Sarawad Castle where the wealthy owner, Doctor the Hon. Eustace Baggeley, was in permanent residence. It would be true to add, though, that the Doctor was often away in the sense that he was in the habit of taking strange drugs prescribed by himself. Morphine, heroin and mescalin had been mentioned but Sarsfield believed that the injections were a mixture of the three, plus something else. Like Ned Hoolihan, the Doctor was also a pioneer of a kind. And, again like Ned Hoolihan, he had adopted Sarsfield, another orphan and born in Chicago, when he was attending a medical conference in that city on the extraction by cattle of a toxic, hypnotic drug from hay imported from Mexico.

After Tim had cleared away his breakfast things and washed the dishes, he went up the stone stairs, accompanied by Corny, to refurbish the Boss's quarters, array the great four-poster bed in clean linen, sweep floors, dust the handsome sitting-room, light fires and pull the chain in the lavatory. In the bathroom he thoughtfully laid out some spare shaving gear of Ned's, and even put a fishing rod and unloaded shotgun leaning in a corner of the sitting-room. Orders were orders, and Crawford MacPherson would not only be welcome but would be made to feel he was genuinely welcome. It was time, Tim said to himself, that he did a little real work for a change—for he was a conscientious young man. And taking counsel with Sarsfield would have to wait for a little bit.

The forenoon passed quickly and it was about two o'clock in the early autumn day when Tim sat down to his heaped dinner of cabbage, bacon, pulverised sausage and sound boiled potatoes of the breed of Earthquake Wonder—with *Jude the Obscure* by Thomas Hardy propped up against the milk jug. Corny dined noisily on a large ham-bone which originally bore rags of meat. Some people, Tim reflected as he finished his food, thought Hardy a rather repressed and dismal writer, more taken with groans than lightness of the heart. Well, he was long-winded all right but the problems he faced were serious, they were human questions, deep and difficult, and the great Wessex novelist had brought to them wisdom, solace, illumination, a reconciliation with

♣ 27 ♣

God's great design. And he had re-peopled the English countryside. The volume itself was the property of Mr Hoolihan.

A grinding metallic noise came from the courtyard and, looking through the thick distorting glass of the narrow window, Tim saw the leading part of the bonnet of a large motor car. He knew a good deal about cars, and had driven and looked after a Lancia when Ned Hoolihan was in residence.

'Humph,' he muttered. 'A Packard. Ex-inventory for years. Drive a Packard and proclaim yourself an old man.'

But he sat there, unmoved. Could this be the Scotchman? Or maybe a manure vendor? Corny growled softly. Whoever it was, he could knock, no matter if the door was only the tradesman's entrance. Even if it was Jude the Obscure he could knock.

But there was no knock.

The door was noisily flung inward and framed in the entrance was an elderly woman clad in shapeless, hairy tweeds, small red-rimmed eyes glistening in a brownish lumpy face that looked to Tim like the crust of an apple-pie. The voice that came was harsh, and bedaubed with that rumbling colour which comes from Scotland only.

'My name is Crawford MacPherson,' she burred rudely, 'and am I to understand that you are Tom Hartigan?'

'Tim.'

'Tom?'

'Tim!'

'Whatever your name is, tell that cross-bred whelp to stop showing his teeth at me.'

'My name is Tim Hartigan, the dog's is Corny, ma'm, and both of us are harmless.'

She moved forward a few steps.

'Don't you dare to call me ma'am. You may call me

MacPherson. Have the manners to offer me a chair. Have you no respect for weemen or are you drunk?'

As Tim Hartigan rose, *Jude the Obscure* fell from his fingers to the floor.

2

PERHAPS IT was a result of Tim Hartigan's alacrity and good humour, but Crawford MacPherson's mood softened somewhat to one which, though still formidable, was not ferocious. From her big handbag she took a flat silver flask and from it poured yellowish liquid into an empty glass on Tim's table. Corny affected a watchful sleep and Tim, busy loading his pipe, had taken a seat on a chair near the window. MacPherson was looking round what once upon a time had been a considerable kitchen, and grimacing as she sampled her drink.

'How are things going on here?' she asked at last.

'Well, ma'am ... MacPherson, I mean ... going on pretty all right. They are nearly ready for harvest, we have three heifers—two of them milkers—ten bullocks, fifty-five sheep, a saddle horse, three tractors, about twenty-five tons of turf and timber, a few good farm workers, and there is a shop about a mile away for groceries, newspapers, fags and that sort of thing ... And there's a telephone here but it's usually out of order.

'I suppose you think that's very satisfactory?'

'Well . . . I suppose things could be worse. The owner, Mr Hoolihan, has made no complaints.'

'Oh, is that so? Do you tell me that?'

Here Crawford MacPherson seemed to frown balefully at the floor.

'I think that's the truth,' Tim replied rather lamely, 'but it's only rarely that I get a letter from him.'

MacPherson put her glass down noisily.

'Let me tell you something about Mr Edward Hoolihan, Hartigan,' she said sternly. 'I'm his wife.'

'Good Lord!' cried Tim, colouring.

'Yes,' she continued, 'and don't you dare call me Mrs Hoolihan. I am not compelled by civil or Presbyterian canon law to make a laughing-stock of myself with a title the like of that.'

Tim shifted uneasily in his chair, his mind in disarray.

'Aw, well . . . I know,' he began.

'I'm over here to put into effect a scheme of my own which, however, has my husband's full approval. There is, of course, no limit to the amount of money I can spend. Mr Hoolihan thinks that nothing can be done about the peasants of this confounded country. Well, about that, we shall see. *We shall see!*'

Tim Hartigan could suspect storm clouds in his future; some thunder. Even lightning, perhaps.

'Mr Hoolihan,' he said gently, 'had some trouble with them himself some years ago. He found them too conservative. He offered them good advice and material help in agriculture but, bedamn it, they wouldn't take it. You see, they're stick-in-the-muds, MacPherson.'

'Ah', she said taking another sup from her glass, 'stick-in-the-muds? Yes, they had no time for Earthquake Wonder, I'm told. I'll tell you this much. Stick-in-the-muds they may be, but my business here is to make sure that it is in their own mud they will stick. Understand me? *In their own mud!*'

'Yes. They're unlikely to want to do anything else.'

Crawford MacPherson rose, strode to the range where a fire glowed, and turned her back to it, standing menacingly in her brown brogues.

'What they want or don't want is not the important thing, Hartigan. It wasn't, in the past, when a terrible potato famine swept through the country like the judgment of God, about 1846.'

'Ah well,' Tim ventured, 'that was in the dim dark days in the long ago, before we had the good fortune to have Earthquake Wonder in the world.'

MacPherson shook her forefinger in anger.

'The people of this country,' she thundered, 'live on potatoes, which are 80 per cent water and 20 per cent starch. The potato is the lazybones' crop and when it fails, people die by the million. They are starving . . . and they try to eat nettles . . . and straw . . . and bits of stick, and they still die. But a more terrible thing than that happened last century . . .'

'Heavens above,' Tim cried, 'what worse calamity than that could occur?'

'The one that *did* occur. They didn't all die. Over a million of those starving Irish tinkers escaped to my adopted country, the United States.'

'Thank God,' Tim murmured devoutly.

'Yes, you can thank your God. They very nearly ruined America. They bred and multiplied and infested the whole continent, saturating it with crime, drunkenness, illegal corn liquor, bank robbery, murder, prostitution, syphilis, mob rule, crooked politics and Roman Catholic Popery.'

'Well, the Lord be praised,' gasped Tim, staggered by the violence and suddenness of this outburst.

'Adultery, salacious dancing, blackmail, drug peddling,

pimping, organising brothels, consorting with niggers and getting absolution for all their crimes from Roman Catholic priests . . .'

Tim frowned.

'Well, a lot of other foreigners emigrated to the States,' he said. 'Germans, Italians, Jewmen . . . even those Dutchmen in baggy trousers.'

'People from the European mainland are princes compared with the dirty Irish.'

'Oh, I say,' Tim cried.

He was angry but his feeling of dismay and being at a loss for a devastating answer was greater. How could he deal with this tartar? Was she off her head?

She unexpectedly returned to the chair at the table and plopped down. She drained the remnant in her glass.

'However,' she said, 'I don't expect you to understand these matters or know how serious they are. You were never in the United States.'

Tim coloured deeply and struck his chair-arm.

'Madam, neither was Saint Patrick.'

She opened her bag, produced American cigarettes and lit one.

'I will give you an outline,' she said, 'of the special business that brings me here. The plan will take considerable time to carry out, and I expect your co-operation and assistance. The object is to protect the United States from the Irish menace. The plan will be very costly but I have so much money from Texas oil at my disposal that I fear no difficulty on that score. My first step will be to buy and nominally take over all Irish agricultural land.'

Tim raised his eyebrows, looking sour.

'That would be the highroad to trouble in this country,' he said. 'That famine was partly due to rackrenting and absentee landlordism. The people formed an organisation known as the Land League. One man they took action against was Captain Boycott. That's where the word boycott comes from.'

But MacPherson, unenlightened, pulled at her cigarette thoughtfully.

'Don't imagine for a moment, Hartigan,' she said in her hard voice, 'that I intend to get myself embroiled in Irish politics. If I had any taste in that direction, I would not have to leave America to indulge it. I will buy the land and then let it back to the tenants at a nominal rent. A rent of perhaps a shilling a year.'

'A *shilling* a year an acre?'

'No. A shilling a year for every holding no matter what the size.'

'Well, holy Saint Paul,' Tim muttered in wonder, 'that would make you out to be the soul of generosity altogether, an angel in disguise from the Garden of Eden.'

MacPherson gave a bleak smile.

'There will be one condition, a strict condition. They will not be allowed to grow potatoes.'

'But what are the unfortunate people to live on?'

'What they've always lived on. Starch.'

Tim puckered his cheeks in a swift inaudible intake of breath. What a strange spectre of a woman this was to be sure! Where would her equal be found in the broad wideness of the world?

'There is one thing even more productive of starch than the potato,' she went on. 'And that is sago.'

'What? *Sago?*'

'Yes—sago. Do you know what sago is, Hartigan?'

Tim frowned, ransacking his untidy mind.

'Well . . . sago . . . is a sort of pudding, full of small little balls . . . like tapioca. I suppose it's a cereal, the same as rice. And maybe it is subject to its own diseases, like the spud . . .?'

Again MacPherson's wintry smile came.

'Sago,' she said with a minute sort of civility, 'is not like tapioca, is not a grain, and will stay free of all disease if its growth is watched. Sago comes from a tree, and the sago tree takes between 15 and 20 years to mature before it can yield its copious, nourishing, lovely bounty.'

Tim stared at his boots. The proposition itself was extraordinary, the time complication incredible.

'I see,' he said untruthfully.

'The plan is big,' MacPherson conceded reasonably, 'but in essence reasonable and simple.'

'All the same,' Tim ventured, 'I think you would have to see the Government about it.'

'Well, you *are* smart,' MacPherson said, almost pleasantly. 'That has already been largely taken care of. The American Ambassador in this country has had his instructions. He will shortly inform the Government here that the immigration of Irish nationals to the United States will be prohibited until the cultivation of potatoes in this country is totally banned.'

Tim suspected he could detect a faint suffusion of perspiration about his brow. He was upset by the velocity of coming events, unless the lady was trying to be funny.

'Well now,' he said at last, 'suppose you get all this land as you say, and have the sowing of potatoes declared a crime——'

'Then,' MacPherson interrupted, 'there never again will be a potato famine, and never will there be another invasion of the United States by the superstitious thieving Irish.'

'Yes, I know. But you said it takes a sago tree up to twenty years to be any use. What in the name of God are the people to live on during that long time?'

Again came the smile, small but icy.

'Sago,' she said.

Tim Hartigan groaned.

'I know I'm stupid but I don't understand.'

'Of course I foresaw the question of that gap and have, of course, taken the necessary steps. Beginning in about eight months, my fleet of new sago tankers will ply between Irish ports and Borneo. There are boundless sago reserves, all over the East Indies—in Sumatra, Java, Malacca, Siam and even in South America the cabbage palm is very valuable for sago. Soon you will see sago depôts all over this country.'

Tim nodded, but frowning.

'Suppose the people just don't like sago, like me?'

A very low, unmusical laugh escaped from MacPherson.

'If they prefer starvation they are welcome.'

'Well, how will you get this sago plantation going?'

'Sago trees will grow anywhere, and two freighters loaded with shoots will arrive shortly. A simple Bill in your Parliament expropriating the small farmers and peasants can be passed quickly, with a guarantee that there will be no evictions, or at least very few. You are a young man, Hartigan. You will probably live to see your native land covered with pathless sago forests, a glorious sight and itself a guarantee of American health, liberty and social cleanliness.'

She stood up with some suggestion of conclusion.

'Well, I must get myself fixed up here,' she said. 'Hartigan, will you bring in my horse?'

Tim turned pale. He had already seen from his narrow window that a narrow horsebox was fastened to the rear of the Packard car and had been wondering about it. Surely it must be a pony?

'To the stables, do you mean?' he asked.

'No, in here. I always like to have my horse near the fire.'

Tim got up silently and went out. There seemed to be no limit to this woman's excesses. That night or the following day he would have to get a cable off to Ned Hoolihan for confirmation of these mouthfuls and occurrences, and the assertion that this woman was in fact his wife. He could not have himself made a fool of, or the house destroyed by a lunatic.

A sliding iron vertical bar with bolt at the back of the horsebox was quickly undone and, as the doors opened, Tim's eyes encountered a number of tall, round, smooth, wooden poles, apparently in some way fastened together.

'A clothes-horse by the holy Peter,' he muttered.

He blessed himself, pulled out the apparatus, half-shouldered it and staggered towards the house. In the kitchen he pulled it apart so that it stood up.

'That's a good man,' said MacPherson in genuine approval.

'I must tell you,' said Tim collapsing to his chair, 'that I had a letter from Mr Hoolihan notifying me of your approaching visit and asking me to have his own quarters upstairs made ready for your occupation. I've done that. Your bed is ready and there's a fire in your bedroom. Do you like sausages for your breakfast?'

'Certainly not. My usual breakfast is oaten porridge followed by sago and cream, and with brown bread and country butter.'

Tim managed to nod amiably.

'Well,' he smiled, 'this place we are in is really the kitchen, and more or less where I live myself. Now, this horse. Shall I bring it up to your own fire?'

MacPherson's eyes wandered about the floor in thought.

'Em, I'm not sure. Leave it here for tonight. Get my travelling bag from my car and then show me to my . . . my flat. I'll give you a bag of sago.'

Tim Hartigan did as he was bid. His new charge made no comment at all on Ned Hoolihan's opulent suite but made straight for the lavatory, suggesting to Tim that she had been told where it and everything else was. He scratched his head and stumbled down the stairs, clutching a bag of sago.

'Must get on to Sarsfield as soon as absolutely possible,' he whispered to himself. 'Else I'm absolutely shagged.'

3

'WELL, I'M sorry for your trouble, Tim.'
Sarsfield Slattery was standing with his backside
outwardly poised towards a great log fire, his feet on a
rug of thin brown ropes, knitted by himself. He was of
smallish structure, thin, with moppy fair hair; sharp, perky
features were lit up with narrow, navy-blue eyes, and his
peculiar way of speaking with jerky accent and intonation
was permanent evidence that he had been born in the northern part of Ireland and was to that extent a sort of disguise,
for he had been born in Chicago. The air he carried with him,
whether he liked it or not, was one of ineffable cuteness and
circumspection. Strangers knew that they had to be very
wary with Sarsfield.

It was noon on the rainy morrow. Tim Hartigan lolled
sadly in a cane chair, having given Sarsfield a full account of
Crawford MacPherson's arrival the preceding day, and what
she had said. The recital made things appear much worse
even than they had been and, indeed, a lorry had arrived that
morning with bags and parcels for the lady, contents
undisclosed.

'Weemen,' Sarsfield added, 'can be wee reptiles, do you know.'

Tim had just lit his pipe and looked thoughtful.

'I'm not a windy sort of fellow as you know, Sarsfield,' he said, 'but I don't like the idea of being by myself with *her* in that house. God knows what she'd turn around and do.'

'You can lock the kitchen at night, can't you?'

'At night? Couldn't she get funny ideas during the day?'

'What sort of funny ideas?'

'Couldn't she walk down the stairs without a stitch on her?'

'Ah, I wouldn't say she's that sort.'

'Or write and tell Ned that I came up with her tray in the evening and me ballock-naked?'

'Ned wouldn't swally that sort of story,' Sarsfield said, grimacing as he pulled at his ear. He paused.

'Tell you the truth, I think Ned must have been floothered when he married that one, and then shipped her out of the States as soon as he could to get shut of her. Too bad that you are left holding the baby.'

'I see?' Tim replied gloomily. 'And what do you think of this sago business?'

'It's all balls.'

'That's just what I think, too. But listen here, Sarsfield, if she does get a bit cracked—a bit more cracked than she is— where am I? I have no witness. Now, if she agreed to live *here* . . . instead?'

Sarsfield's answering look was piercing.

'Holy God, isn't a married woman entitled to live in her husband's home?'

Tim coloured a little.

'I suppose so. I've no proof that she's his wife.'

'Hasn't she got a ring? What takes *me* to the fair is your brave notion of unloading her on this house. Haven't we enough trouble here? If you have no thought for me, you would be foolish to take anything for granted about my lord and master, Dr the Honourable Eustace Baggeley.'

'Oh, I know I'd have to consult the Doctor, Tim. How is he, by the way?'

'He's happier than ever, which means he's worse. He's taking his doses twice a day now. He is talking about converting this castle into a luxury hotel, and even having a casino here. The tourist trade, you know. He thinks the Americans are very attractive people because, like himself, they all seem to have a lot of money. Not that they spend it, if you ask *me*.'

Tim frowned a little, clutching at a wisp of hope.

'Is that so? Faith and he might take an interest in Mrs MacPherson. Why not? She's the wife of one of his best friends and she says she's absolutely stinking and crawling with money.'

'Thank goodness they *are* very good friends,' Sarsfield said acidly. 'That's a very good reason why the Doctor should keep very far away from that lady.'

'Oh, I don't know. The Doctor's not a lady's man, if that's what you mean. What the hell is that hammering, Sarsfield?'

Sharp noises, somewhat muffled but loud enough, were heard from the upper intestines of the Castle.

'Ah, that? That's Billy Colum, the handyman. The Doctor gave him orders to put up a framework of timber all around the walls of the big return-lounge, and cover it all over with teak panelling. He's the job nearly finished, and the lounge ruined. I think that's the first stage in the hotel-casino project.'

'Good Lord, Sarsfield.'

'Aye. The Doc will destroy himself pumping that stuff into his arm. And I think he gives Billy Colum an odd dart now and again.'

'Could I see the Doctor? I think I should tell him about

♣ 43 ♣

Mrs Ned. You can be sure she's bound to know of him, Sarsfield. I'd better mark his card.'

'Whatever you say, Tim. As far as I know he's above in the library. You know the way. Off you go.'

Tim did know the way but paused at the lounge to observe Billy at his extraordinary job. A void about four feet wide remained in a large long apartment without the pale shiny panelling already in place from floor to ceiling, built on a heavy timber framework about a foot from the original ornate walls.

'That's a great feat of intricate construction, Billy,' Tim said.

Billy Colum, a wizened, wild-eyed little man, looked about him as if seeing his handiwork for the first time.

'Do you know, Tim' he said in his low hoarse voice, 'I think the poor Doc is going a bit batty at last. As well as this how-are-ya, he told me to keep an eye out for any jewels that might be knocking about the Castle. He says they can be picked up anywhere.'

'Jewels?'

'Jewels. Big ones.'

'Does he ever give yourself any medical treatment?'

'Certainly he does. My rheumatism. He gives me a little pain-killer in the arm here. Mind you, he's a good doctor behind it all. How could I lift my arm to use a hammer without him?'

Tim smiled as he moved on.

'A casino will be a great improvement in this part of the world,' he remarked.

4

THE LIBRARY at Sarawad Castle wore its name sombrely but correctly. A noble, elongated, high-ceilinged room, it had lofty windows which looked strangely narrow, along the right hand, with a single one at the far end corresponding with the door—all hung with dark red curtains, and on those three sides the dark spines of books rose on shelf after shelf from the floor to the roof. In the middle of the fourth wall was a great mantelpiece of green-veined black marble, with brass fire-dogs at the hearth, and a conflagration of steam coal and logs blazing in the grate. Some chairs and other small furniture stood near the fire and, somewhat removed from it in the upper half of the room, was a wide, low, distinguished desk. Between it and the fire was a leather armchair in which sprawled elegantly Doctor the Hon. Eustace Baggeley.

The Doctor was quite stout, with ample black hair plastered down, and a middle parting over his broad head. His clean-shaven fleshy features were rude and genial, and his general air was of that kind of youthfulness which warns the perceptive that the man wearing it cannot be as young as he appears. His dress was seen to be fastidious and expensive as he rose to greet Tim Hartigan.

'My dear boy,' his low cultured voice said as he stood up with his hand out, 'do please come in and sit down. Well, well, Tim, and how are we?'

Tim smiled, shook hands and sat down.

'I'm very well indeed, Doctor. Nothing to complain about that I can think of.'

'That's the stuff. All at cookhouse orders, as we used to say in my Army days. And how is Master Cornelius?'

'Oh, in grand form, Doctor. Still at all-out war with all the rats in the parish.'

'Excellent.'

'I was over seeing Sarsfield, Doctor, and I thought I'd come up here and have a little chat about a few things . . .'

'I am delighted that you did, dear boy. Tell me this. Have you had any recurrence of that fibrositic visitation in the region of the groin?'

'No indeed. No sign of that for months.'

'I am glad. Let me know at once if there should be any more trouble. I have a new embrocation here, administered subcutaneously, a therapeutic truly miraculous straight from Germany.'

Tim spread his hand in polite disclaim.

'Thank God I have no need for anything, Doctor.'

'Too rash an asseveration,' said Dr the Hon. Baggeley, rising and going to a sideboard in the dim recess of the far corner.

'If your health is good, still it cannot be so good that a glass of Locke's of Kilbeggan will not put a fresh gloss on it.'

As he handed over the glass with a slight bow, he excused himself for not being able to *chequer les verres* but his kidneys had advised to abstain for a while. He then passed a little jug of water and sat down again, beaming. Tim recalled hearing that alcohol and strong narcotics were often incompatible. He took a good drink of the strong amber distillate and began to fill his pipe.

'Doctor Baggeley,' he said, 'I wanted to tell you I've had a visitor.'

'A visitor, dear boy?'

'Yes. A very strange one. A Scotch lady.'

The Doctor slapped his knee.

'Well, well. Scotch . . . and a lady? Scotland for ever!'

Tim rammed expertly at his pipe-bowl.

'That's not all, Doctor. She's living with me . . . at Poguemahone Hall.'

'Dear boy! Well, well, well. *Living* with you . . .?'

He rose and paced delightedly to the hearth rug.

'Living with you in mortal sin, in the opprobrious bondage of the flesh?'

Tim managed a weak smile.

'No, Doctor, I didn't say that, but that isn't all either.'

'Don't tell me, dear friend, that she is a distinguished pianist, or somebody that has come to find the True Cross in the Bog of Allen?'

'No. She says she is Ned Hoolihan's wife!'

The Doctor, taken quite off guard in the midst of his banter, staggered to his seat, collapsed into it and presented to Tim a look of blenched amazement. His eyes stayed wide and motionless.

'Ned . . . married . . . to a Scotch shawlie? Heavenly sweet crucified Redeemer and his Blessed Mother above! You are not taking a rise out of me, dear boy?'

'I don't think so, Doctor. I have no proof but that's what she said. And I think she is telling the truth. Her name is Crawford MacPherson and that's what she wants to be called—not Missus Hoolihan.'

The Doctor bowed his head, cradling it in his right hand.

'Dear boy, this is most disturbing but let us keep our heads. I would make a telephone call to Ned tomorrow if we only knew where to find him—the damn fool is always up in aeroplanes all over that dirty Texas oil country. As you know, dear boy, I warned him not to go out there.'

'Yes, I remember. It was foolish, but he made a lot of money.'

'*Money?* Pfff! He had more than he could use when he was here, and what use is money to a man who gets himself married to a Scotch hawsie from the fish-gutting sheds of Aberdeen?'

Tim demurred a bit.

'I don't care for her, Doctor, but I don't think that she's quite that type. I mean, she's no lady but all the same she's not the low working-class type. She brought a horse with her.'

'A horse, Tim? Sacred grandfathers! Why should anybody bring a horse to Ireland, where the brutes are to be found in every hole and corner of the country?'

'It's a wooden horse, a folding affair—I mean a clothes-horse. She made me put this thing in front of my own fire.'

Doctor Baggeley reflectively fingered his jaw.

'I see,' he mumbled. 'Yes. That could—I say could—mean one thing. What we call diuresis.'

'What's that, Doctor?'

'Pathological incontinence. Bed-wetting and all that line of country.'

Tim was dismayed.

'Good Lord! And my friend, poor Ned. Do you mean, Doctor, that she's going to . . . to dry things at my fire instead of upstairs at her own?'

He gulped savagely at his new drink as Doctor Baggeley had risen to pace the floor once again in thought. He stopped.

'Do you know, my dear friend, whether she has any money with her? That itself would be a test of whether she is really Ned Hoolihan's wife. He is, after all, many times a multi-millionaire, even if it's in dollars.'

Tim finished his drink and put his glass on a side table with a click so conclusive that the Doctor absently replenished the glass immediately from the bottle now on the mantelpiece.

'Now listen, Doctor Baggeley,' Tim said collectedly. 'If you would please sit down there again in your chair, I will tell you all I know about Crawford MacPherson's money and her plans.'

'Yes, dear boy.'

Obediently he sat down, calming himself, and lit a cigarette.

'According to herself she has money without end, millions and millions of it, all of which she can spend with the approval of Mr Hoolihan, her husband. It seems she can do what she likes with it but she has a plan, a plan to change the whole face of Ireland.'

'Dear me now. And why is that?'

'Because she hates the Irish.'

'Well, dear boy, that is true of a lot of other people but there is little they can do about it. What particular reason has she for hating the Irish?'

'Because after the Great Famine many, many years ago when the potato crop failed, America was invaded by a million and a half Irish people, starving emigrants if you like, but they pulled through, settled down, and increased and multiplied.'

Doctor Baggeley nodded, admiring Tim's gift of concise exposition.

'Of course it wasn't just this influx itself that annoys Crawford MacPherson. It's what the Irish brought with them and planted in America—things she thinks are terrible and dirty.'

'What sort of things, dear boy? Do you mean dancing to the fiddle—the Rakes of Mallow, the Stooks of Barley and Drive the Jenny Wren?'

'No, no, Doctor. She says they brought drunkenness, and kip-shops full of painted women . . . and pox . . . and the Catholic faith.'

The Doctor made a clucking noise.

'Upon my word, dear boy, but I would not agree that the Irish were pioneers in these matters at all. And the Catholic Church? Heavens above, don't you and I belong to it? And do you remember President Kennedy?'

'Yes. But Crawford MacPherson does not.'

'We have the Knights of Columbanus here, remember. Converting outsiders is their business, and I think they get an indulgence for every soul—forty years and forty quarantines or something of the kind.'

Tim shook his head.

'Crawford MacPherson has a plan, Doctor. An amazing long-term plan. She wants to make certain there never will be another Great Famine in Ireland because of a failure of the potato crop—and indeed that might happen because of the scandalous way the people here turned up their noses at Earthquake Wonder.'

'How right you are, dear fellow. I have tried more than once to persuade Billy Colum and his friends to make Earthquake poteen. That's the boy that would bend your back and make you sing!'

'But,' Tim pursued, 'any potato, she says, is mostly starch. She wants to replace the potato here by sago, which gives even more starch and is far more hardy. Sago is grown on trees. She wants to have forests of sago trees all over Ireland. She wants to buy up all the farming land and make sago compulsory.'

Slow-mounting amazement and pleasure suffused the

large countenance of Dr the Hon. Eustace Baggeley. He almost sprang from his chair to stand on the hearth-rug, bending towards Tim.

'Sago? *Sago?* Ah, dear boy, you bring me back to Sumatra, to my Army days. Sago, by Saint Kevin of Glendalough! My dear boy, the very word sago means *bread*.'

'I don't like it, Doctor.'

'Ah, you may be confusing it with tapioca. You get tapioca by heating the root of the bitter cassava, a tropical shrub of the spurge family. Starch is produced, certainly, but it has nothing to do with sago. Manioc is another name for tapioca.'

'Do you tell me that, Doctor?'

'Yes, my boy. In certain parts of South America, meat and manioc is about the only diet for the natives. And they get by on it, but sago would make men of them.'

Tim's face clouded in some wonder.

'Do you think, Doctor, that sago trees could be grown here?'

'Of course, dear boy. Of course. Why not? Haven't we got the Gulf Stream? Heavens above, I am delighted!'

'Delighted?'

'I am charmed. Perhaps it is because I am a military medical man but did you know that the Brazilian Indians discovered that roasting the tubers of cassava would disperse the hydrocyanic acid in the milky white sap?'

'No, but is that why you are delighted?'

'Well, not quite, but the manioc shrub grows quickly anywhere, and kills weeds. My heart, though, is in sago.'

Tim pulled at his pipe. He found it rather difficult to pin the Doctor down, and now Crawford MacPherson had been momentarily forgotten. The Doctor had moved to a rather littered medicinal tray on his desk and was genially selecting among the contents.

'My dear boy,' he said, 'I hope to see again, but in Ireland, the gilded palaces of Siam, the turrets and domes of Malacca and pavements littered with baked cakes of sago . . . ah, the wild, burnished enchantment of the East . . .'

He had found simultaneously an ampoule and a hypodermic syringe.

'But Crawford MacPherson,' Tim urged, 'says that growing those trees will take years?'

The Doctor had given himself an injection on the side of the right buttock, putting the needle through the trouser cloth. He then sat down, pleased.

'A sago palm of the right strain, my dear Tim,' he said, 'can mature in fifteen years.'

'Well,' Tim rejoined, 'she says she is going to import sago to this country in tankers, to feed the people while the trees are growing, and wean them off potatoes!'

The Doctor beamed but his face was slightly vacant, reflective.

'I must immediately meet this interesting and gallant lady, Tim. She would now be in Poguemahone Hall, I suppose. But before I go it is essential that you yourself should be instructed in this new big thing, a thing that will change radically the history of Ireland and later the whole social tilt of Western Europe. Have you ever heard of Marco Polo?'

Another stranger, Tim thought. Wasn't the Scotch lady enough to be going on with for the present?

'I don't think so, sir,' he said coolly.

'Well, there are books here. Now let me see . . .'

He rose and walked steadily to the loaded shelves, searching with his eyes, touching the spines of books with questing finger. Two he took down and paused, looking for a third.

'You see,' he said with back still turned, 'even if it takes a tree fifteen years or more to mature, *you have only a given ten days or so within which to fell it.* You must fell it when it first

breaks into bloom, otherwise all your sago is lost. It all goes to
nourish the flowers. Do you understand, my dear boy?'

He had returned to his chair, putting three books on the
desk and examining one of them.

'Well, if that's the situation, Doctor,' Tim said expansively, 'the trees would have to be spread out as to the times
of planting, otherwise you could have tens of thousands of
trees requiring to be felled almost on the same day . . . and
where would you get the labour in a situation like that?'

The Doctor smiled in approval.

'How very alert you are,' he said. 'Splendid! I think Ned's
good wife will have an able lieutenant in you. Yes. Now I'm
marking certain pages and passages in these books with slips
of paper. I want you to take a rest here and read those
passages: here, I mean, today. And read also any other parts
which may appeal to you. You may rely to an unlimited
extent in your labours on the produce of Locke's Distillery of
Kilbeggan.'

He rose, as did Tim also, surprised.

'But,' he asked, 'what about my new boss at the Hall?'

The Doctor patted his shoulder.

'You need not worry about that at all, my dear boy, for I
am now on my way to see her. I will explain that I have
asked you to undertake some research that would be dear to
her heart. So sit down and relax, and have another drink. On
my way down I will see Billy Colum is getting on with that
panelling in the hall. And I'll tell Sarsfield not to disturb you
here but to bring you up a tray in a few hours.'

Tim Hartigan smiled. He knew this man could be quite
impossible but his heart was in the right place.

'Well, thanks, Doctor,' he said. 'That's very nice of you.
I'll do what you say. But I would like you to warn Sarsfield
Slattery about one thing.'

'What is that?'

'No sago.'

'Ah-ha? No sago.'

With a wave the Doctor was gone, carrying a very small bag.

5

Tim Hartigan, having picked up the first book, went back to his chair and looked it over. Good large print, he noted with approval. Opening it at the bookmark finally, he laid it face down and attended meticulously to his glass, pouring himself a generous noggin of Locke's medicament, flavouring it slightly with water and then gratefully flushing his gullet downward. No wonder, he reflected, that the old-time monks were great scholars, for they had the wit to make on the premises the medicine that gave the mind ripeness and poise, satisfying the bodily thirst while sharpening the thirst for knowledge on that wine from the butts of God's vineyards of human knowledge

He eyed the library about him with a friendly eye, then carried his book and vessels to the great desk and thankfully sank into the commodious personal chair of Doctor the Hon. Eustace Baggeley. Then he began his reading.

Sleator's Deposit of Dietetic Cosmography, p. 627:
The true sago palm flourishes in low marshy situations, growing to a maximum height of thirty feet. It matures to yield starch at age 15 to 20 years.

The whole interior of the stem will then be found to be gorged with spongy medullary matter enclosed by a hard shell—the only wood of the stem. At this stage the tree will be observed to put forth its terminal flowering spikes and after three years, these ripen to fruits and seeds. If this is allowed to proceed, the whole starch will have been used up, the stem becomes a hollow shell, and the plant has been killed in that supreme effort. But immediately the flowering spikes appear, the stem is felled, cut up into portions of from four to six feet long, and carried off to the factory.

There they are split lengthways, and their medullary starch scooped out. This is thrown into water and washed until all fibrous material and other impurities float to the surface. After standing for a time, the fecula settles on the bottom of the trough, and is successively washed and the water decanted. Then it is dried and constitutes 'sago meal'.

To prepare for the shops the meal is again moistened and put into bags, in which it can be well shaken and beaten when suspended from the roof of the room.

It is next rubbed over sieves of various mesh until it is separated into 'pearl sago', 'granulated sago', etc, when it is dried in the open or over ovens.

The refining of sago into the grades required by the European market is done largely by the Chinese in Singapore . . .

About 1913 the average yearly imports to the United Kingdom of sago, sago meal and sago flour was about 29,000 tons.

♣   ♣   ♣

The Book of Marco Polo the Venetian (2 vols.)
by Col. Sir Henry Yule. Vol. II, p. 300:

The people have no wheat, but have rice which they eat with milk and flesh. They also have wine from trees such as I told you of. And I will tell you another great marvel. They have a kind of trees that produce flour, and excellent flower it is for food. These trees are very tall and thick but have a very thin bark, and inside the bark they are crammed with flour. And I tell you that Messer Marco Polo, who witnessed all this, related how he and his party partook of this flour made into bread, and found it excellent.

Ibid., pp. 304–5:

An interesting notice of the sago tree, of which Odoric also gives an account; Ramusio is however here fuller and more accurate: 'Removing the first bark, which is but thin, you come upon the wood of the tree, which forms a thickness all round of some three fingers, but all inside this is a pith of flour, like that of the Carvolo. The trees are so big that it will take two men to span them. They put this flour into tubs of water, and beat it up with a stick, and then the bran and other impurities come to the top, while the pure flour sinks to the bottom. The water is then thrown away, and the cleaned flour that remains is taken and made into *pasta* in strips and other forms. These Messer Marco Polo often partook of and brought some with him to Venice. It resembles barley bread and tastes much the same. The wood of this tree is like iron, for if thrown into water it goes straight to the bottom. It can be split straight from end to end like a cane. When the flour has been removed the wood remains, as has been said, three inches thick. Of this the people make short lances, not long ones, because they are so heavy that no one could carry or handle them if long. One end is sharpened and charred in the fire and, when thus prepared they will pierce any armour, and much better than iron would do.'

♣ ♣ ♣

Malay Archipelago 1896 by A. E. Williams:
When sago is to be made, a full-grown tree is selected just before it is going to flower. It is cut down close to the

ground, the leaves and leaf-stalks cleared away and a broad strip of the bark taken off the upper side of the trunk. This exposes the pithy matter, which is of a rusty colour near the bottom of the tree, but higher up pure white, about as hard as a dry apple, but with woody fibres running through it about a quarter of an inch apart. The pith is cut or broken down into a coarse powder, by means of a tool constructed for the purpose . . .

Water is poured on the mass of pith, which is kneaded and pressed against the strainer till the starch is all dissolved and has passed through, when the fibrous refuse is thrown away, and a fresh basketful put in its place. The water charged with sago passes to a trough, with a depression in the centre, where the sediment is deposited, the surplus water trickling off by a shallow outlet. When the trough is nearly full, the mass of starch, which has a slight reddish tinge, is made into cylinders of about thirty pounds' weight, and neatly covered with sago leaves, and in this state is sold as raw sago. Boiled with water, this forms a thick glutinous mass, with a rather astringent taste, and is eaten with salt, limes and chillies. Sago bread is made in large quantities, by baking it into cakes in a small clay oven containing six or eight slits, side by side, each about three-quarters of an inch wide and six to eight inches square. The raw sago is broken up, dried in the sun, powdered, and finely sifted. The oven is heated over a clear fire of embers, and is lightly filled with sago powder. The openings are then covered up with a flat piece of sago bark, and in about five minutes the cakes are turned out sufficiently baked. The hot cakes are very nice with butter, and when made with the addition of a little sugar and grated cocoa-nut, are quite a delicacy. They are soft, and something like corn-flour cakes, but have a slight character-istic flavour which is lost in the refined sago we use in this country. When not wanted for immediate use, they are dried for several days in the sun, and tied up in bundles of twenty. They will then keep for years; they are very hard, and very rough and dry.

Tim closed the book, finished the remains of his drink and thoughtfully re-charged his glass. He frowned a little as he filled his pipe. How could people seriously attempt to live on sago? Is it really a staple, such as bread made from wheaten flour is with us? And would those easterly people think it very odd that the Irish should put such trust in potatoes, even if the potatoes were (as assuredly they were not) Earthquake Wonders? By all accounts the Garden of Eden was not marshy and it was fairly sure that no lofty sago trees there kept off the heat of the sun, any more than Adam and Eve dug the sinless soil for the world's first potatoes. He kindled the pipe and half-closed his eyes in reverie.

The door flew inward with a noise and Sarsfield Slattery hurried inward, alert and frowning a bit.

'Tim, was Billy Colum here?'

'No. Nobody was here. Why?'

'I was bringing him a cup of tea and a slice of brown bread. The Doctor told me to keep an eye on him. He's gone!'

'*Gone?* Heavens, I was just reading some stuff here about sago to please the Doctor, and, well . . . thinking . . . and drinking. I thought Billy was working away down there.'

'Well, he has disappeared off the face of the earth. The Doctor is at your place. I'd better ring him'.

Tim nodded helplessly.

'I suppose it would be the wise thing,' he agreed.

6

A T POGUEMAHONE HALL Tim decided to leave Sarsfield
and go up to Crawford MacPherson's private quarters
alone. His own life having so swiftly proceeded from
simplicity to complexity, he now began to fear boundless
confusion and resolved for his own part to be more than
careful. What untold things might not result from the collision
of the drug-charged Doctor and a foreigner with no right
command of her wits? What incomparable things might
happen in the house of Ned Hoolihan while the owner was
up in an aeroplane mapping his oil empire in Texas or
marking the spot of a rogue gusher? Tim knocked on the
door and entered.

Dr the Hon. Eustace Baggeley was elegantly sprawled on the
broad sofa, smiling broadly with a gleam in his eyes. Crawford
MacPherson was in the armchair by the fire: not annoyed,
not genial but seemingly in an acceptable neutral humour.

'Well, Tim, what's the trouble?' she asked.

'My dear boy, you look pale,' the Doctor beamed.

Tim ventured to take a seat, for his own ingestion of
Locke's had somewhat dissipated his natural reticence.

'I thought I should let you know Doctor, that your man Billy Colum has disappeared. Sarsfield Slattery missed him and after we searched and shouted for him, we thought we should come over here and let you know right away.'

MacPherson put the glass in her hand on the table.

'What's this, Doctor? People disappearing? Innocent bodies being whisked away? I thought things were settled in this country.'

The Doctor airily waved a hand.

'My dear Crawford, nothing in this world is ever settled. Billy is a queer little man, full of whims and crucified with rheumatism. He'll probably show up again in a few days. Maybe he has gone to see his old mother in Killoochter. Did he leave a message, Tim?'

'He left nothing, sir. Just disappeared.'

MacPherson stood up.

'It seems it is just my misfortune to walk into some sort of criminality at your Castle, Doctor. A thing that smells of agrarian kidnapping, Fenianism or something of the kind. Where are the police? I can ring up the American Ambassador in Dublin if there is a telephone in working order in this unholy district.'

The Doctor also rose, intact in his good humour.

'My dear lady, nothing of the kind. Billy is quite harmless, and a first-class carpenter. He was panelling a hallway for me. We don't keep office hours in this country, you know. You never can tell. He might have suddenly remembered that he had to post a letter and there's a two-mile walk in that job.'

The lady snorted.

'I have no doubt at all,' she said in a hard voice, 'that your wretched potatoes inflict weakness in the head as well as in the bones. All the same, he is your workman, Doctor. We had better go and investigate.'

'But, my dear Crawford . . .'

'At once!'

In a surprisingly quick time coats and hats had been got and the company, including Sarsfield Slattery, were getting into the Doctor's aged Bentley. Nothing could disturb his panache and, as the car started, he gave his new passenger caution of what to expect from the unkempt country roads of Ireland, even if the journey was less than a mile.

'I am not a complete tyro, Doctor,' she replied. 'I got off the liner near Cork and drove up here in my Packard, and it couldn't be worse in the highlands of Kangchenjunga. Why haven't the people here smart ponies and traps instead of those donkey-carts?'

'Ponies,' replied the Doctor, 'are useless for agricultural labour in the little fields. We need all-purpose animals here, and cars that can carry potatoes and manure as well as people. In my Army days outside Singapore we had plough-ing done by cows. Did you ever eat yak butter, Crawford?'

'I did not, Sir. I take it you have never heard of sago butter?'

The Doctor laughed.

'Indeed no, but though delicious, like sago cheese, it's hardly as nourishing as cows' butter.'

'*Nourishing?* That's the nonsense to be heard from doctors all over the world—*nourishing*. Are potatoes nourishing? The purpose of food is to keep people alive, *and in their own country*. Potatoes are hardly known at all in the States. It is surprising how easy it is for the Irish who get there to forget their native spuds.'

'That reminds me,' Sarsfield interjected. 'Billy Colum missed his dinner.'

The Doctor had been driving his gallant old car and was now nearing his own splendid castellated entrance, always hospitably open, with the pushed-back gates permanently immured in stones and bracken.

'Here we are at Sarawad, Crawford. The word sarawad is Gaelic and means "before long". A delightful name, you'll agree. It spells out hope, and better times to come.'

Looking about her the lady said:

'There's a lot of loose, foolish talk out of the people here—all of them. The climate may take part of the blame but not all of it. I hope you have a drink in the house, Doctor?'

The Doctor had pulled up and reached for the doors.

'Here we are, madame. Sarawad Castle, home of peerless foodstuffs and the true, the blushful Hippocrene.'

Crawford MacPherson did not waste time or admiration on the fine old door or the lofty entrance hall, nor on the gaming weapons and animals' heads which crowded its walls; she seemed to be leading the party, as if she owned the Castle, up the stairs to the lounge which had been the scene of Billy's labours. The artificial walls of teak, flawless and complete, gleamed in the evening light while a chair, a saw and the neat mess a good carpenter leaves behind were in the middle of the floor.

'He was finishing the job here as I passed down,' the Doctor said tapping a section of the wall. 'I gave him a little bit of a hand and he appeared to be his usual good self.'

'Was he sober?' MacPherson asked.

'Sober as the day he was born because Billy never touched intoxicating drink. It wasn't that drink was against his rule, or mine either, but it played hell with his rheumatism. You see, his rheumatism was congenital, the poor man. He was a martyr to that disorder but he never complained nor let himself be depressed.'

'He offered all his pains up to God,' Tim said piously.

MacPherson glowered about the room and from face to face.

'How could a cripple be a carpenter?' she demanded.

'Oh, the Doctor himself looks after him,' Sarsfield replied. 'He gets by all right, ma'am.'

'Don't you dare call me ma'am!'

'You see, Crawford,' the Doctor interposed, 'his trouble is not really old-fashioned inflammation of the muscles and joint tissue but a verruculose affection of the tendons. Very disabling and discouraging but a dart from me restores him to condition, rather like winding up an alarm clock. You may be sure I look after my staff.'

'I see. His muscles are all right but his tendons are permanently wrecked. I imagine that situation would make him worse. Has he been given to disappearing like this?'

'Not really, Crawford,' the Doctor replied amiably. 'But he takes his own time at a job, and goes about it in his own way. You see, we're a sort of happy family here. Billy Colum was a bit of an artist. You can't hurry a man of that kind—not if you want a proper stylish job done.'

'And tell me, Doctor, do those injections sicken or upset him in any way?'

'Yerra not at all. They sometimes make him sing, help to take him out of himself. Help him to get a good night's sleep, too, for he does have a touch of insomnia.'

'But does he eat properly?'

'Lord save us,' Tim interrupted, '*eat?* He's so hungry most days he'd eat a dead Christian Brother. When Billy sits down he clears the decks. Give him a bucket of Irish stew—potatoes, onion and any God's amount of meat, boiling hot, and he'll shovel it down the inside of his neck like a man possessed.'

MacPherson glared at him.

'You mean, young man, that he is addicted to gluttony? Doctor, could we pay a visit to your own quarters, just the two of us?'

'A pleasure, Crawford.'

Tim and Sarsfield looked at each other ruefully as their betters departed. This lady made as little distinction as

☘ 65 ☘

between persons and classes. She was just as overbearing and peremptory with the Doctor as with them and apparently thought her husband's money had demolished all barriers.

'This ould wan,' Sarsfield mused, 'is getting a bit on my nerves.'

'Is that so, my poor man,' Tim rejoined drily. 'This is the first time she has been here, possibly the last time. I have to live with her, day and night, and she may be staying at Poguemahone for years—*for years*, man. How would you like changing places with me?'

'I'd rather go to the States, like Hoolihan. But Billy . . . I know that the Doc sometimes gives him a dart of his own needle. Something terrible is going to happen. I didn't hear Billy leave the house, in fact I didn't miss him till I went to call him for his dinner.'

'What's all the fuss about?' Tim asked irritably. 'He finished his job. He finished his job and maybe decided to slope off for a drink. You heard the Doc say that Billy was a total abstainer? That was a good one.'

'Listen, Tim,' Sarsfield said earnestly, 'you know very well Billy doesn't get ideas of that kind. When he's tired working and hungry, the only idea in his head is to make a ferocious attack on his dinner. You know that very well.'

Tim did not pay much attention, for he was examining and testing the panelling—a job well done, he had to confess, and skilfully.

'Let's hope,' he said at last, 'that Billy won't be found drowned in a bog hole.'

'Does her ladyship let you smoke?' Sarsfield asked.

'What?' Tim rasped. 'Me, smoke? I'll smoke my pipe any time and anywhere I want to.'

Sarsfield lit a cigarette and pulled gratefully at it, undeterred by returning voices.

'Since you have the instrument, my dear,' the Doctor said

re-entering, 'you might give the chests of those two boys a run over. They are divils for smoking, a thing I personally steer clear of. Any news, boys?'

'Not a thing,' Tim said as he noticed that MacPherson was swinging a stethoscope.

'Holy God,' muttered Sarsfield taken aback.

'Show me again, Doctor,' MacPherson said briskly, 'just where the missing man finished his work.'

'Surely,' the Doctor replied. 'I stopped to talk to him and gave him a slight amateur's helping hand just here, look.'

She nodded and, with ear-pieces in place, began to run the bell of the stethoscope over that particular part of the wall, stooping to cover the lower parts. Suddenly she stood upright and wheeled round.

'You,' she said sharply to Tim Hartigan, 'get a chisel or something and break the panelling away at this seam!'

Frowning, Tim bent among the tools. The Doctor, still jovial but a little concerned, intervened.

'But, my dear, that's finished work—I mean, it would be a pity to break it up.'

Tim carefully handed a chisel and hammer to Sarsfield.

'Quite so, Doctor. It would also be a pity for one of your workmen to lose his life.'

After a nod from his employer, Sarsfield inserted the chisel-edge at a scarcely perceptible seam and began his crude hammering until rending sounds concluded with a ragged gap torn in the panelling. MacPherson peered in.

'Quick, boy,' she cried, 'break down some more towards the floor and get him out. He's in there, on his back!'

Confusion of work and voices ensued until Tim found himself behind the panelling dragging the comatose Billy to his feet and manhandling him towards the light of the ope—and final rescue.

'Well, good Lord,' the Doctor said gaping, 'how on earth

could he build himself into the wall? The tiny nails are driven in from the outside. Goodness me, this is the limit. How do you feel, Billy?'

MacPherson, hands on huge hips, was grim.

'Doctor, did you help him with this job? Did you give him an injection for his tendons?'

Billy was sitting disconsolately on the floor, only partially conscious.

'He's coming to,' Sarsfield cried.

'I certainly gave him a little help,' the Doctor said pleasantly. 'That verruculose affliction could put a delicate job like this all wrong.'

'You'd better put this man to bed,' MacPherson said to Sarsfield, 'and then let us have a rest in your library, Doctor.'

'With pleasure, my dear,' the Doctor replied with total recall of his good humour. 'Those careless little chaps would need somebody to mind them all the time.'

At first undecided, Tim followed his principals to the library, happy that he had earlier put away his own books and drinking utensils. MacPherson sat by the fire, putting the stethoscope on the desk while the Doctor produced the Locke's and three—yes, three—glasses. MacPherson drank appreciatively, apparently judging that the situation was one of some small triumph for her.

'My dear Doctor,' she said, 'forgive me if my manner over this little mystery seemed a bit brusque. But human suffering disturbs me. That is why I feel that the money at my disposal must be applied to the amelioration of man's lot in general.'

'By the ingestion of sago, my dear?'

'That is one way, the fundamental way for Ireland. But it is not by any means exclusively a matter of the stomach, of diet, or even of the startling change in the national scenery. With vast countrywide plantations of sago pine there will be, for example, a new wild life in Ireland . . .'

The Doctor clapped hands.

'My dear girl, how charming! You do excite me. In my Army days—indeed, in all my younger days—the hunt was a preoccupation with me which almost made my work take second place. I never enjoyed shooting at people, mattera-damn whether they were niggers or coolies . . . but tigers! Ah!'

MacPherson contrived the ghost of a smile.

'Well, in my own younger days,' she said, 'researching sago in the wilder parts of Sumatra and the Malay Peninsula, I had to be on my guard against some very large fierce creatures such as the Asiatic elephant, the bison and the rhinoceros, and several kinds of bear . . .'

'Jolly good, by Jove!'

'But these large mammals would scarcely find sustenance in Ireland, even if they were allowed to kill and eat the people. But the smaller wild animals can be deadlier. The sago rat is indigenous in any territory where the pine grows. The tapir, the sambhur and the siamang, a strange sort of anthropoid ape, will probably appear here. Also the crab-eating macaque, I can see that flourish in Connemara. I would not be sure of the Asiatic tiger and black panther coming here, for they are very wide-ranging and predatory creatures, but many smaller jungle cats and wild boars may be expected. There would be no counting the breeds of alien birds which would roost in the sago pines . . .'

'Ah, my dear lady—blue partridge, argus pheasant and the cotton teal, I sampled them in the eating-houses of Hong Kong.'

'Yes, Doctor, but a thing not to be ignored will be the swarms of new insects, house-monkeys and quadruped snakes and, glory be to God, the din will be something new to this country, particularly at night.'

There was a brief silence of reflection.

'Are you sure, my dear Crawford, that this ... this bouleversement of hemispheres, to so speak, is worthwhile in the mere interest of changing the potato for sago in this country?'

MacPherson put down her empty glass smartly.

'Of course I do. Don't millions of people live under such conditions in the East? What would happen if they were all to decide to emigrate to America?'

'Hmmm. That would be a bad show. Have another drink?'

'Thanks.'

'Tim?'

'Thank you, Doctor.'

'I must be getting home, Doctor, very soon. I have letters to write and notes to make. So charming meeting you.'

The Doctor beamed genuinely.

'Ah, my dear Crawford, for me it has been a supreme pleasure and honour to welcome to these poor parts the wife of my dear friend Edward Hoolihan. I will ask Sarsfield Slattery to drive you home in my car.'

'But thank you so much. We will meet again in a few days. I want to talk to you about another most important by-product. I mean sago furniture.'

And thus a meeting, so strange in its sequel, came to an end that evening.

7

On reaching Poguemahone Hall, Tim Hartigan parted from the new chatelaine, picked up in the hall an airmail letter addressed to himself and made his way to his kitchen quarters. He was tired, and intestinally a bit irked by spent whiskey. He went to bed, rekindled his pipe and opened the letter.

DEAR TIM — It's beginning to be the devil out here. More gushers are blowing their tops about every third day and I don't believe I manage a total of more than fifteen hours real sleep a week, quite alone and in perfect peace, peace that was possible only by reserving an entire floor of the Blue Water Gulf Hotel in Corpus Christi with a squad of my own private cops to keep Press and TV scruff away and to block all telephone assaults. It's not that I'm short of assist- ance and offers of help. Those offers are so continuous and persistent and descending on me from every quarter in such a deluge that my nerves by now are pretty well in flitters. A Jesuit Father, Michael Peter Connors, managed to get him- self invited up to breakfast with me on the pretext of getting a sub for a new convent of the Little Sisters of the Stainless

Eucharist in Dallas (of course I'm still as much of a sucker for the old Church as ever I was as a simple farmer at Poguemahone) and when he pulled out some sort of an illuminated book for me to sign so that I would be remembered in 10,000 Masses that are to be offered in the convent chapel for benefactors over twenty-five years from the opening date, a little box of ·357 Smith and Wesson slugs fell out into his damn plate of bacon. I knew them and the box because I have one of those rods myself. I pressed a secret buzzer at my foot under the table and when two cops bounced in and frisked my Jesuit he turned out to be a cousin of Congressman Joshua Hedge—a real friend of mine in Washington, I think. This silly bogman didn't plan to shoot me, of course; he just wanted a cheque, no matter a bugger to whom payable, so as to have some notes to play with and maybe buy himself a vacation in Europe. I gave him fifty bucks in notes but warned him I'd give Hedge a prod about him. It looks to me like everybody in this Texas goes about fully armed and any man in the habit of carrying readies in his pocket has a quiet bodyguard about as near to him as his underwear—he wouldn't go to the lavatory without a gunman on guard outside the door. I needn't tell you I carry an old-fashioned Colt 45 myself *and know how to use it*—got lessons and half an hour's practice every day for a fortnight from the Marshal at Fort Worth, a Clareman named O'Grady. I carry a couple of grut balls, too—little bombs about a thousand times worse than tear gas but with no effect on the thrower (yours truly) who takes just one grutomycin tablet every morning. Don't write to me here in Corpus Christi as my G.H.Q. is still Houston. I have moved from the Old Mexico mansion and now have seven floors in the Houston Statler, and please make a note of that address. George Shagge, the Laredo steel-man, wants me to buy the whole damn hotel and settle in but I don't know, I think I'll wait a bit. Some of my oil tickles in Arizona have suggested that this State is sitting on a bed of uranium and maybe Texas won't be my last home. But I like it here. This territory is so big and so bulging with treasure under the ground that a man feels he's neglecting it just by being in any one place. Oil means hundreds of miles of big-bore pipeline, some to my refinery at Houston and others to new refineries I am putting up at Galveston and Sabine, and also at Pensacola in Alabama—we can't move oil to the west and east coasts except by tanker. The railroads here are all in the hands of crooks. I've taken over a firm making drilling rigs in Tulsa, Oklahoma, for by jiminy I have options on 1,858 sq. miles of fresh territory here in Texas where the tests have been more than good. Total no. of H.P. derricks at work just now is 731. Two fellows I know here are running for Governor in the neighbouring State of New Mexico—Cactus Mike Broadfeet and Harry Poland—and I'm quietly backing both because that's the way business goes here. This whole State is alive with hoodlums and politicians, and when was there any difference between those two classes? I'm as busy as buggery but I'm not slow—I play the Kennedy R.C. ticket and I'll be just another brave U.S. Catholic as soon as my citizenship comes through—Cactus Mike says I'm perfectly right and that this great State of over seven million souls is entitled to a Cardinal and if he is elected Governor in New Mexico he intends to park some fixers and use money (mine, I presume) in Rome. By God, if he wants to serve the Cross that way, why shouldn't he since he serves or used to serve the fiery cross with the K.K.K. outfit—and now with an election next door there's no shortage of those gunboys in nightshirts putting the fear of Jesus into the niggers. You might think I'm now long enough in the U.S.A. to have a few friends here and there but honestly, Tim, I'm lonely as hell and have to keep fighting like a trojan to keep away from the licker. Some of my buddies, as they call themselves, may be all right under the skin but I just don't have the mental machinery to tell which of them are bums or hoods. They have all a profound, sincere, undisguised interest in money—MY money, I'd say—and I needn't tell you they mostly want it to prop up poor prostitutes in homes, teach the alphabet to blind cripples, found new Orders of nigger and octaroon nuns and make absolutely certain that the Democrats will never lose this State. Cactus Mike Broadfeet has a button up certifying he has given 24 pints to the Our Lady of the Lake Blood Bank at San Antonio but maybe the button means he swallows 24 pints of corn licker a week for by God you'd swear his face was on fire. As I think you know, the only way to get about this territory which is bigger than all Germany is by air. I've two machines of my own, a jet and a turbo-prop but I'm nervous as a kitten up there, even if every flyer and cop I have took an oath on the Douai to play straight. Four of my boys have been shot up in the last ten months and a girl that types for me got so savagely mugged that the New York hospital that now has her says she'll never walk or stand up again. The mobsters here have no respect whatsoever for womankind. With a State election coming up nearby the night riders have got mighty plentiful and Harry Poland has made the crack on TV that Cactus Mike Broadfeet would be the ideal man for Governor of Oklahoma except that he has trench mouth, his love for the Democrat Party is a phoney, he has a bordello in the sacristy of his First American Church of the Plymouth Presbyterians *and* his expectation of life is short—that last a thing Poland has referred to the Attorney as a threat of assassination. Somehow I feel Cactus Mike will pull this thing off because he is a real prairie Texan, owns a big chain of shirt factories through the west coast and the word has been spread that Harry Poland is a Jew from Lithuania, though he wears a holy medal in gold he got from Cardinal Spellman and never touches meat on Friday. He has cotton scrubshops at Austin, Amarillo and El Paso but the boys say his real call is the drug business and that he was linked up with the Mafia outfit Cosa Nostra. He certainly takes snow himself for the good of his health and that's about the colour of his face if not of his soul. Do you know, I'm nearly mad enough to run for the chair of Governor of one of the States here only I'm not a citizen yet. What I DO wish badly is that yourself could come out here and give me a hand at running this big booming oil mess-up but of course you can't with all that important work on your hands back there at Poguemahone. By God though I need a real Irishman out here. Things will be easier later on though, when I get some sort of a real *organisation* working—that's the big, true, business word, ORGANISATION. By the Lord, we have enough juice hereabouts to oil the wheels if only we had the wheels there and organised to turn.

Now Tim I've left to the last the big question never out of the back of my distracted mind these times—*how is my dear wife Crawford?* I'm sure you were pretty shook and maybe annoyed with me for the abrupt way I unloaded her on you without any right warning but Tim, you could say that girl saved my life when this sudden oil strike unbalanced me and drove me straight to the bottle. In three months I was half-way down the river on a tide of bourbon, not even the decent potstill drop you have at home, giving orders in the oil fields, signing options and cheques and hiring and firing without any proper notion of what I was about. God in his mercy saw to it that Crawford was lurking somewhere on my office staff and He inspired her to come to my side, guide my silly hand, save me from myself and get me the best doctors to be had across the whole U.S.A. and a first class specialist named Dr Feodor Unterholtz from Austria. She never took her eyes off me nor let anybody else mess me up, and one night even had the nerve to order Cactus Mike out of the house. An angel in disguise if you like but still an angel. And she did not pull back when a direct sacrifice by herself was called for. As you probably know by now she is of stern Presbyterian stock but knew I would never be permanently safe, safe for keeps, unless she married me. You can well imagine the awful struggle that was there in the middle of her soul for of course she knew I was an Irish Catholic and knew the view our sort of people take of the sacrament of marriage. See the hobble she was in? I think she saw Cardinal Spellman or Cardinal Cushing or somebody on the Q.T. but I can tell you this—when the awful choice was put in front of her on a plate, Crawford didn't flinch. No, sirreee! She took instruction from a local P.P., learned her prayers like a Castlebar schoolgirl and behind my back was received into the Church. Another soul for God, Tim—aren't they wonderful, the ways of Providence? I was on tegretol and morphine and benzedrine and the devil knows what but I nearly fell through the middle of the bed when she told me one night everything was fixed. It made a new man of me, invalid and all as I was. I made a novena of thanksgiving to Our Lord and His Blessed Mother, and I don't give a damn how much cynical people will jeer at all the oil and money I have, there was no trouble at all to getting Cardinal Cushing to agree to give us a Solemn Pontifical Nuptial High Mass with Gregorian Choir for the wedding. I arranged a sort of a double-take by having the Mass, wedding ceremony and the reception at the Houston Statler brought live on closed-circuit TV to the New York Hilton where a second simultaneous reception was held, with Senator Hovis Oxter and his wife Bella deputising for myself and bride, and I think you can take it from me that a good time was had by all—or by about 7,500 guests. Our honeymoon at Miami was very brief, of course, and very *careful* indeed with myself on antabus if you know what that drug is for, sweet God the smell of a cork and the poor reformed drinking man is down the Swanee.

I suppose you wonder what I think of Crawford's brain-storm about putting an end for good and all to potato-eating in Ireland. Well, this America is a great country with nothing beyond the boundless horizon only another enormous horizon beckoning on but I still remember very affectionately the land that gave me birth but I may say that the disgraceful way the native peasants treated my Earthquake Wonder still rankles bitterly in my nose. If the Irish don't recognise a sound, decent, bug-free potato when they are offered one, then they don't deserve any potato at all—those are *my* feelings—and they have thoroughly merited the decision to have sago made the national mainstay. Poor Crawford tried to interest myself in sago but nothing in that line has ever agreed with me, though who can say what I would think at my present age if I had had sago from the cradle as the new generation of Irish people probably now will have. My own conviction and my money are totally behind Crawford's scheme because (one) the extremely delicate and complicated business of handling oil-men, geological and mineral technicians, banker and financial panjandrums, to say nothing of State and Federal politicians, *are no proper concern for a decent young married woman*: and (two) my dear wife is finding happiness in the fulfilment of philanthropic yearnings far from home. It is a great pleasure and consolation to me that she should decide to see the bigger world from the resolve, God willing, to improve it and in doing so help me to discharge honourably the burdens of the great wealth which has flowed to me, and that keeps flowing in an ever-rising tide, from the Texas soil. There are not many dedicated persons in this shabby old world, and Crawford

Hoolihan is one of them. Ireland may yet salute her, with holy Saint Brigid and Queen Maeve and the other great ladies of our storied past, not forgetting Graunya Wayl. I thank God humbly that she is far away from the hurly-burly and prairie stink of Texas oil, for nobody can pretend that gasoline is a pretty thing. And listen, Tim—don't be fooled if it seems for the present that she doesn't care a damn about you and takes you just for a gobshite of a caretaker. *I marked her card* and made it plump and plain that in my book you were the decentest and ablest young Irishman who ever wore a hat. I told her you were a sort of son of mine, though I didn't labour that point. Crawford doesn't wear her heart on her sleeve but she is far too shrewd to make any mistake about a man like you or even our mutual friend Sarsfield Slattery. Ah, how is Sarsfield? There is one little point I would like you to look to with your special care. Crawford has all the charity, humility and simplicity of a Saint Francis of Assisi or a Saint Teresa of Avila in her little finger but there is one thing she has yet to learn something about: I mean TACT. God help us but her honest direct attitude and methods might give offence to some of the over-sensitive slobs who still abound in Ireland's green and pleasant land. There is, if you like, something of the Saint Joan about her. Give her some help and guidance there, Tim! Never tire telling her that the Irish are easy-going (you and I know that they are just bone-lazy) and that it is far easier to lead them gently than to push them. I need hardly tell you that she has plenty of the proper contacts in high places, and I had Senator Hovis Oxter introduce her to old Mrs Scheisemacher, mother of the American Ambassador in Dublin, Charlie Bendix Scheisemacher. I might tell you under the hat Charlie is a stockholder and not a tiny one either in my H.P. Petroleum outfit and I can pull his whiskers any time I want to. You will find that Crawford will move fast as soon as she gets her bearings and if she has told you that she has already arranged to ship sago to Ireland in tankers as a stop-gap measure, it is perfectly true because she arranged it all through my own tanker subsidiary. I'm telling you, she'll wake Ireland up—and about time!

Do write to me, Tim, and tell me what is going on and how things are shaping. What impression has Crawford made on my native sod? How many local people has she met? What does Sarsfield Slattery think of her? And my old sparring partner Baggeley, how is he behaving and has he yet heard any tidings of my wife? My hope is that they won't meet, because the Doctor's health habits make him rather unreliable. The enclosed little extra cheque, which you need not mention to Crawford, is for yourself. Write, write, WRITE, Tim, and give me all the news. *Yours ever — Ned.*

(At this point the original manuscript ends.)

The Martyr's Crown

M R TOOLE and Mr O'Hickey walked down the street together in the morning.

Mr Toole had a peculiarity. He had the habit, when accompanied by another person, of saluting total strangers; but only if these strangers were of important air and costly raiment. He meant thus to make it known that he had friends in high places, and that he himself, though poor, was a person of quality fallen on evil days through some undisclosed sacrifice made in the interest of immutable principle early in life. Most of the strangers, startled out of their private thoughts, stammered a salutation in return. And Mr Toole was shrewd. He stopped at that. He said no more to his companion, but by some little private gesture, a chuckle, a shake of the head, a smothered imprecation, he nearly always extracted the one question most melodious to his ear: *'Who was that?'*

Mr Toole was shabby, and so was Mr O'Hickey, but Mr O'Hickey had a neat and careful shabbiness. He was an older and a wiser man, and was well up to Mr Toole's tricks. Mr Toole at his best, he thought, was better than a play.

And he now knew that Mr Toole was appraising the street with beady eye.

'Gorawars!' Mr Toole said suddenly.

We are off, Mr O'Hickey thought.

'Do you see this hop-off-my-thumb with the stick and the hat?' Mr Toole said.

Mr O'Hickey did. A young man of surpassing elegance was approaching; tall, fair, darkly dressed; even at fifty yards his hauteur seemed to chill Mr O'Hickey's part of the street.

'Ten to one he cuts me dead,' Mr Toole said. 'This is one of the most extraordinary pieces of work in the whole world.'

Mr O'Hickey braced himself for a more than ordinary impact. The adversaries neared each other.

'*How are we at all, Sean a chara?*' Mr Toole called out.

The young man's control was superb. There was no glare, no glance of scorn, no sign at all. He was gone, but had left in his wake so complete an impression of his contempt that even Mr Toole paled momentarily. The experience frightened Mr O'Hickey.

'Who . . . who was *that?*' he asked at last.

'I knew the mother well,' Mr Toole said musingly. 'The woman was a saint.' Then he was silent.

Mr O'Hickey thought: there is nothing for it but bribery—again. He led the way into a public house and ordered two bottles of stout.

'As you know,' Mr Toole began, 'I was Bart Conlon's right-hand man. Bart, of course, went the other way in 'twenty-two.'

Mr O'Hickey nodded and said nothing. He knew that Mr Toole had never rendered military service to his country.

'In any case,' Mr Toole continued, 'there was a certain day early in 'twenty-one and orders come through that there was to be a raid on the Sinn Fein office above in Harcourt Street. There happened to be a certain gawskogue of a cattle-jobber from the County Meath had an office on the other side of the street. And he was well in with a certain character be the name of Mick Collins. I think you get me drift?'

'I do,' Mr O'Hickey said.

'There was six of us,' Mr Toole said, 'with meself and Bart Conlon in charge. Me man the cattle-jobber gets an urgent call to be out of his office accidentally on purpose at four o'clock, and at half-four the six of us is parked inside there with two machine-guns, the rifles and a class of a home-made bomb that Bart used to make in his own kitchen. The military arrived in two lurries on the other side of the street at five o'clock. That was the hour in the orders that come. I believe that man Mick Collins had lads working for him over in the War Office across in London. He was a great stickler for the British being punctual on the dot.'

'He was a wonderful organiser,' Mr O'Hickey said.

'Well, we stood with our backs to the far wall and let them have it through the open window and them getting down off the lurries. Sacred godfathers! I never seen such murder in me life. Your men didn't know where it was coming from, and a lot of them wasn't worried very much when it was all over, because there was no heads left on some of them. Bart then gives the order for retreat down the back stairs; in no time we're in the lane, and five minutes more the six of us upstairs in Martin Fulham's pub in Camden Street. Poor Martin is dead since.'

'I knew that man well,' Mr O'Hickey remarked.

'Certainly you knew him well,' Mr Toole said, warmly. 'The six of us was marked men, of course. In any case, fresh orders come at six o'clock. All hands was to proceed in military formation, singly, be different routes to the house of a great skin in the Cumann na mBan, a widow be the name of

Clougherty that lived on the south side. We were all to lie low, do you understand, till there was fresh orders to come out and fight again. Sacred wars, they were very rough days them days; will I ever forget Mrs Clougherty! She was certainly a marvellous figure of a woman. I never seen a woman like her to bake bread.'

Mr O'Hickey looked up.

'Was she,' he said, 'was she . . . all right?'

'She was certainly nothing of the sort,' Mr Toole said loudly and sharply. 'By God, we were all thinking of other things in them days. Here was this unfortunate woman in a three-storey house on her own, with some quare fellow in the middle flat, herself on the ground floor, and six blood-thirsty pultogues hiding above on the top floor, every manjack ready to shoot his way out if there was trouble. We got feeds there I never seen before or since, and the *Independent* every morning. Outrage in Harcourt Street. The armed men then decamped and made good their excape. I'm damn bloody sure we made good our excape. There was one snag. We couldn't budge out. No exercise at all—and that means only one thing . . .'

'Constipation?' Mr O'Hickey suggested.

'The very man,' said Mr Toole.

Mr O'Hickey shook his head.

'We were there a week. Smoking and playing cards, but when nine o'clock struck, Mrs Clougherty come up, and, Protestant, Catholic or Jewman, all hands had to go down on the knees. A very good . . . strict . . . woman, if you under-stand me, a true daughter of Ireland. And now I'll tell you a damn good one. About five o'clock one evening I heard a noise below and peeped out of the window. Sanctified and holy godfathers!'

'What was it—the noise?' Mr O'Hickey asked.

'What do you think, only two lurries packed with military,

with my nabs of an officer hopping out and running up the steps to hammer at the door, and all the Tommies sitting back with their guns at the ready. Trapped! That's a nice word—*trapped*! If there was ever rats in a cage, it was me unfortunate brave men from the battle of Harcourt Street. God!'

'They had you at what we call a disadvantage,' Mr O'Hickey conceded.

'She was in the room herself with the teapot. She had a big silver satteen blouse on her; I can see it yet. She turned on us and gave us all one look that said: *Shut up, ye nervous lousers.* Then she foostered about a bit at the glass and walks out of the room with bang-bang-bang to shake the house going on downstairs. And I seen a thing . . .'

'What?' asked Mr O'Hickey.

'She was a fine—now you'll understand me, Mr O'Hickey,' Mr Toole said carefully; 'I seen her fingers on the buttons of the satteen, if you follow me, and she leaving the room.'

Mr O'Hickey, discreet, nodded thoughtfully.

'I listened at the stairs. Jakers I never got such a drop in me life. She clatters down and flings open the halldoor. This young pup is outside, and asks—awsks—in the law-de-daw voice, "is there any men in this house?" The answer took me to the fair altogether. She puts on the guttiest voice I ever heard outside Moor Street and says, "Sairtintly not at this hour of the night; I wish to God there was. Sure, how could the poor unfortunate women get on without them, officer?" Well lookat. I nearly fell down the stairs on top of the two of them. The next thing I hear is, "Madam this and madam that" and "Sorry to disturb and I beg your pardon," "I trust this and I trust that," and then the whispering starts, and at the wind-up the halldoor is closed and into the room off the hall with the pair of them. This young bucko out of the Borderers in a room off the hall with a headquarters captain of the Cumann na mBan! *Give us two more stouts there, Mick!*'

'That is a very queer one, as the man said,' Mr O'Hickey said.

'I went back to the room and sat down. Bart had his gun out, and we were all looking at one another. After ten minutes we heard another noise.'

Mr Toole poured out his stout with unnecessary care.

'It was the noise of the lurries driving away,' he said at last. 'She'd saved our lives, and when she come up a while later she said "We'll go to bed a bit earlier tonight, boys; kneel down all." That was Mrs Clougherty the saint.'

Mr O'Hickey, also careful, was working at his own bottle, his wise head bent at the task.

.   .   .   .

'What I meant to ask you was this,' Mr O'Hickey said, 'that's an extraordinary affair altogether, but what has that to do with that stuck-up young man we met in the street, the lad with all the airs?'

'Do you not see it, man?' Mr Toole said in surprise. 'For seven hundred year, thousands—no, I'll make it millions—of Irish men and women have died for Ireland. We never rared jibbers; they were glad to do it, and will again. But that young man was *born* for Ireland. There was never anybody else like him. Why wouldn't he be proud?'

'The Lord save us!' Mr O'Hickey cried.

'A saint I called her,' Mr Toole said, hotly. 'What am I talking about—she's a martyr and wears the martyr's crown today!'

John Duffy's Brother

STRICTLY SPEAKING, this story should not be written or told at all. To write it or to tell it is to spoil it. This is because the man who had the strange experience we are going to talk about never mentioned it to anybody, and the fact that he kept his secret and sealed it up completely in his memory is the whole point of the story. Thus we must admit that handicap at the beginning—that it is absurd for us to tell the story, absurd for anybody to listen to it and unthinkable that anybody should believe it.

We will, however, do this man one favour. We will refrain from mentioning him by his complete name. This will enable us to tell his secret and permit him to continue looking his friends in the eye. But we can say that his surname is Duffy. There are thousands of these Duffys in the world; even at this moment there is probably a new Duffy making his appearance in some corner of it. We can even go so far as to say that he is John Duffy's brother. We do not break faith in saying so, because if there are only one hundred John Duffys in existence, and even if each one of them could be met and questioned, no embarrassing enlightenments would be forthcoming. That is because the John Duffy in question never left his house, never left his bed, never talked to anybody in his life and was never seen by more than one man. That man's name was Gumley. Gumley was a doctor. He was present when John Duffy was born and also when he died, one hour later.

John Duffy's brother lived alone in a small house on an eminence in Inchicore. When dressing in the morning he could gaze across the broad valley of the Liffey to the slopes of the Phoenix Park, peacefully. Usually the river was indiscernible but on a sunny morning it could be seen lying like a long glistening spear in the valley's palm. Like a respectable married man, it seemed to be hurrying into Dublin as if to work.

Sometimes, recollecting that his clock was fast, John Duffy's brother would spend an idle moment with his father's spy glass, ranging the valley with an eagle eye. The village of Chapelizod was to the left and invisible in the depth but each morning the inhabitants would erect, as if for Mr Duffy's benefit, a lazy plume of smoke to show exactly where they were.

Mr Duffy's glass usually came to rest on the figure of a man hurrying across the uplands of the Park and disappearing from view in the direction of the Magazine Fort. A small white terrier bounced along ahead of him but could be seen occasionally sprinting to overtake him after dallying behind for a time on private business.

The man carried in the crook of his arm an instrument which Mr Duffy at first took to be a shotgun or patent repeating rifle, but one morning the man held it by the butt and smote the barrels smartly on the ground as he walked, and it was then evident to Mr Duffy—he felt some disappointment—that the article was a walking-stick.

It happened that this man's name was Martin Smullen.

He was a retired stationary-engine-driver and lived quietly with a delicate sister at Number Four, Cannon Row, Parkgate. Mr Duffy did not know his name and was destined never to meet him or have the privilege of his acquaintance, but it may be worth mentioning that they once stood side by side at the counter of a public-house in Little Easter Street, mutually unrecognised, each to the other a black stranger. Mr Smullen's call was whiskey, Mr Duffy's stout.

Mr Smullen's sister's name was not Smullen but Goggins, relict of the late Paul Goggins, wholesale clothier. Mr Duffy had never even heard of her. She had a cousin by the name of Leo Corr who was not unknown to the police. He was sent up in 1924 for a stretch of hard labour in connection with the manufacture of spurious currency. Mrs Goggins had never met him, but heard that he had emigrated to Labrador on his release.

About the spy glass. A curious history attaches to its owner, also a Duffy, late of the Mercantile Marine. Although unprovided with the benefits of a University education—indeed, he had gone to sea at the age of sixteen as a result of an incident arising out of an imperfect understanding of the sexual relation—he was of a scholarly turn of mind and would often spend the afternoons of his sea-leave alone in his dining-room thumbing a book of Homer with delight or annotating with erudite sneers the inferior Latin of the Angelic Doctor. On the fourth day of July, 1927, at four o'clock, he took leave of his senses in the dining-room. Four men arrived in a closed van at eight o'clock that evening to remove him from mortal ken to a place where he would be restrained for his own good.

It could be argued that much of the foregoing has little real bearing on the story of John Duffy's brother, but modern writing, it is hoped, has passed the stage when simple events are stated in the void without any clue as to the psychological and hereditary forces working in the background to produce them. Having said so much, however, it is now permissible to set down briefly the nature of the adventure of John Duffy's brother.

He arose one morning—on the 9th of March, 1932—dressed and cooked his frugal breakfast. Immediately afterwards, he became possessed of the strange idea that he was a train. No explanation of this can be attempted. Small boys sometimes like to pretend that they are trains, and there are fat women in the world who are not, in the distance, without some resemblance to trains. But John Duffy's brother was certain that he *was* a train—long, thunderous and immense, with white steam escaping noisily from his feet and deep-throated bellows coming rhythmically from where his funnel was.

Moreover, he was certain that he was a particular train, the 9.20 into Dublin. His station was the bedroom. He stood absolutely still for twenty minutes, knowing that a good train is equally punctual in departure as in arrival. He glanced often at his watch to make sure that the hour should not go by unnoticed. His watch bore the words 'Shockproof' and 'Railway Timekeeper'.

Precisely at 9.20 he emitted a piercing whistle, shook the great mass of his metal ponderously into motion and steamed away heavily into town. The train arrived dead on time at its destination, which was the office of Messrs Polter and Polter, Solicitors, Commissioners for Oaths. For obvious reasons, the name of this firm is fictitious. In the office were two men, old Mr Cranberry and young Mr Hodge. Both were clerks and both took their orders from John Duffy's brother. Of course, both names are imaginary.

'Good morning, Mr Duffy,' said Mr Cranberry. He was old and polite, grown yellow in the firm's service.

Mr Duffy looked at him in surprise. 'Can you not see I am a train?' he said. 'Why do you call me Mr Duffy?'

Mr Cranberry gave a laugh and winked at Mr Hodge who sat young, neat and good-looking, behind his typewriter.

'Alright, Mr Train,' he said. 'That's a cold morning, sir. Hard to get up steam these cold mornings, sir.'

'It is not easy,' said Mr Duffy. He shunted expertly to his chair and waited patiently before he sat down while the company's servants adroitly uncoupled him. Mr Hodge was sniggering behind his roller.

'Any cheap excursions, sir?' he asked.

'No,' Mr Duffy replied. 'There are season tickets, of course.'

'Third class and first class, I suppose, sir?'

'No,' said Mr Duffy. 'In deference to the views of Herr Marx, all class distinctions in the passenger rolling-stock have been abolished.'

'I see,' said Mr Cranberry.

'That's communism,' said Mr Hodge.

'He means,' said Mr Cranberry, 'that it is now first-class only.'

'How many wheels has your engine?' asked Mr Hodge. 'Three big ones?'

'I am not a goods train,' said Mr Duffy acidly. 'The wheel formation of a passenger engine is four-four-two—two large driving wheels on each side, coupled, of course, with a four-wheel bogey in front and two small wheels at the cab. Why do you ask?'

'The platform's in the way,' Mr Cranberry said. 'He can't see it.'

'Oh, quite,' said Mr Duffy, 'I forgot.'

'I suppose you use a lot of coal?' Mr Hodge said.

'About half a ton per thirty miles,' said Mr Duffy slowly, mentally checking the consumption of that morning. 'I need scarcely say that frequent stopping and starting at suburban stations takes a lot out of me.'

'I'm sure it does,' said Mr Hodge, with sympathy.

They talked like that for half an hour until the elderly Mr Polter arrived and passed gravely into his back office. When that happened, conversation was at an end. Little was heard until lunch-time except the scratch of pens and the fitful clicking of the typewriter.

John Duffy's brother always left the office at one thirty and went home to his lunch. Consequently he started getting steam up at twelve forty five so that there should be no delay at the hour of departure. When the 'Railway Timekeeper' said that it was one thirty, he let out another shrill whistle and steamed slowly out of the office without a word or a look at his colleagues. He arrived home dead on time.

We now approach the really important part of the plot, the incident which gives the whole story its significance. In the middle of his lunch John Duffy's brother felt something important, something queer, momentous and magical taking place inside his brain, an immense tension relaxing, clean light flooding a place which had been dark. He dropped his knife and fork and sat there for a time wild-eyed, a filling of potatoes unattended in his mouth. Then he swallowed, rose weakly from the table and walked to the window, wiping away the perspiration which had started out on his brow.

He gazed out into the day, no longer a train, but a badly-frightened man. Inch by inch he went back over his morning. So far as he could recall he had killed no one, shouted no bad language, broken no windows. He had only talked to Cranberry and Hodge. Down in the roadway there was no dark van arriving with uniformed men infesting it. He sat down again desolately beside the unfinished meal.

John Duffy's brother was a man of some courage. When he got back to the office he had some whiskey in his stomach and it was later in the evening than it should be. Hodge and Cranberry seemed preoccupied with their letters. He hung up his hat casually and said:

'I'm afraid the train is a bit late getting back.'

From below his downcast brows he looked very sharply at Cranberry's face. He thought he saw the shadow of a smile flit absently on the old man's placid features as they continued poring down on a paper. The smile seemed to mean that a morning's joke was not good enough for the same evening. Hodge rose suddenly in his corner and passed silently into Mr Polter's office with his letters. John Duffy's brother sighed and sat down wearily at his desk.

When he left the office that night, his heart was lighter and he thought he had a good excuse for buying more liquor. Nobody knew his secret but himself and nobody else would ever know.

It was a complete cure. Never once did the strange malady return. But to this day John Duffy's brother starts at the rumble of a train in the Liffey tunnel and stands rooted to the road when he comes suddenly on a level-crossing—silent, so to speak, upon a peak in Darien.

Thirst

by
Myles na Gopaleen

Characters in the play

MR C.   *A Publican*

JEM ⎫
PETER ⎭   *Customers*

THE SERGEANT

(The curtain goes up on the bar. It is after hours. Light from a distant street-lamp shines faintly on the window. The bar is lit (very badly) by two candles which are set on the counter, one of them stuck in a bottle. The Publican, MR C., who is suitably fat and prosperous in appearance, is leaning over the centre of the counter talking to PETER, who is sitting on a stool side-face to the audience. JEM, who is in the nature of a hanger-on, is away in a gloomy corner where he can barely be discerned. Both customers are drinking pints; the Publican has a small whiskey. The curtain has gone up in the middle of a conversation between PETER and the Publican.)

MR C. *(dramatically)* And do you know why? *(There is a pause.)* Do you know why?

PETER Begor, Mr Coulahan, I couldn't tell you.

MR C. *(loudly, lifting a bottle and pouring)* Because he's no good—that's why—no bloody good at all! *(Finishes pouring bottle.)* And another thing—*(Dramatic pause.)*
    (He finishes his drink in one gulp. Turns to the shelves for the whiskey bottle and noisily fills himself another. As the

talk proceeds he is occupied with pulling two further stouts to fill up the customers' glasses. PETER *smokes and bends his head reflectively.* JEM *is silent save for drinking noises. He shows his face for a moment in the gloom by lighting a cigarette.*)

MR C. He has a brother from the County Galway that comes up every year for the Horse Show, a hop-off-my-thumb that you wouldn't notice passing you on the stairs, all dressed out in fancy riding-breeches. Last year he turned up in the uncle's pub beyond in Drumcondra, complete with fountain-pen . . . and cheque-book. Gave your man as his reference. (*He pauses ominously.*) My God, the unfortunate bloody uncle. (*He laughs hollowly.*) The poor unfortunate bloody uncle. Twelve pounds fifteen shillings he was stuck for. Thirteen pounds you might say—thirteen pounds that he spent a good month of his life gathering together by the sweat of his brow! Now for God's sake—did you ever hear anything like it?

JEM (*who has a strong Dublin accent*) Oh, the cheque-book is the man. Manny's the time I wished to God I had one of me own!

PETER (*slyly*) Of course, that crowd digs with the other foot. It's a lot of money to be stung for, there's no doubt. Some publicans are very foolish.

MR C. Digs with the other foot? If you was to ask me—they dig with both feet! Whatever suits their book at the time, they'll dig with that one. And they do all the digging in other people's pockets! (*Sips whiskey.*) Sure, I believe your man's wife was up for lifting stuff out of Slattery's.

PETER (*surprised*) Is that so? I didn't hear that.

MR C. Certainly, man. Certainly she was.

JEM Begob, half the town's wheelin' stuff outa that place night and day, they do be bringing' hand-carts up there, some of them.

PETER (*reflectively*) It's funny how some families seem to go all the one way. It's some sort of a streak. It's in the blood, I suppose.

JEM Aye, it's the blood right enough.

PETER There's a bad ugly streak in that crowd—although every one of them got a good education. All at the Christian Brothers, no less.

MR C. (*turns to bottle behind him and pours himself another whiskey*) Don't be talking man! Sure it's up in Mountjoy jail I'd have every one of them, and that's where they'll be yet,—doing a stretch of seven years apiece for grand larceny and robbery and thievery and every crime in the calendar. And wasn't there another brother that skipped to America after sticking up a bank in the Troubles—all in the name of Ireland. (*He moves to cash register.*)

JEM Begob, Mr Coulahan, and I forgot about the bank stick-up!

MR C Sure we put up with far too much in this country. (*Sighs.*) And there's a certain other gentleman comes in here for his pint that ought to be locked up too, a very . . . very . . . respectable . . . gentleman—— (*He breaks off.*) What was that? (*Noise.*)

JEM Eh, what's that?

PETER (*startled*) What? I heard nothing.

(COULAHAN *moves to shelves.*)

MR C. Shhh! Shhh! For God's sake! It's the Guards!

PETER and JEM The Guards! The Guards! Begob! We're ruined! (PETER *and* JEM *duck behind counter.*)

MR C. Shhh.

(*He blows out one of the candles, completely obliterating* JEM. *He tiptoes to the window and listens with bent head.*)

MR C. (*in agitated whisper*) Shhh! Now for God's sake. I think that bloody Sergeant is on the prowl.

JEM Begob! We're bunched! (*He blows out candle on table.*)

MR C and PETER Shhh! (*Three knocks on the door.*)

SERGEANT (*outside door*) Guards on duty! Guards on duty. Will you please open up, Mr Coulahan.

PETER We'll keep very quiet.

MR C. (*loudly, in violent agitation*) SHHHHH.

(*There is complete silence.* PETER *leans over to the remaining candle and caps the flame in his hands to hide the lights.* MR C. *is bent nearly double in his intent listening and keeps on Shhh-ing and waving a hand for even further silence. There is no sound at all without. Thirty seconds pass. Suddenly* MR C. *leaps at the candle and blows it out, leaving nothing visible save the window that is lit by the street-lamp. Almost simultaneously three loud knocks are given on the door.*)

(*The knocks are repeated, more urgently. The three remain completely still. Then* COULAHAN *moves to the counter where he finishes his drink. The knocks are given again. The bottom of the door is kicked slightly and the thick brogue of the* SERGEANT *is faintly heard shouting something.* MR C. *is heard sighing heavily.*)

MR C. Well, that's that, that's that. (*He is groping for his matches, finds them and carefully lights both candles.*) Yes, that's that.

(*The knocks are repeated even louder. He comes from behind the counter. Then moves to the door.*)

MR C. Alright, Sergeant, I'm coming. (*He opens the door.*) Good night to you, Sergeant. That's a hardy cold one for you.

SERGEANT (*to invisible Guard*) That's all right, Guard.

(SERGEANT *enters.* COULAHAN *closes door, switches on light.*)

SERGEANT It is, indeed, as you say, Mr Coulahan, a cowld, raw class of a night. 'Tisn't a seasonable time of the year at all for this time of year. 'Tis not indeed!

MR C. (*coming forward with a show of forced gaiety and going back behind the counter*) Well, we can't complain, we had an easy enough winter up till now. No, we can't complain. We can't . . . complain.

(*The* SERGEANT *has found his note book and pencil.*)

SERGEANT It's in the wife's name, if I'm not mistaken, Mr Coulahan?

MR C. Yes, Sergeant, the house is in the wife's name. (*Pause.*)

PETER You know my name, I suppose, Sergeant?

SERGEANT I do. I do. And if I'm not altogether mistaken, that's another old friend of mine beyant.

JEM Oh, too true, Sergeant. Manny's the time we've met before. And will again, please God.

SERGEANT O faith we will. We'll meet again, and many a time. Many a time.

JEM I suppose, Sergeant, you wouldn't mind if I finished me bottle of stout? We don't want waste in these hard times, do we?

SERGEANT (*turning away from* JEM's *direction with great deliberation*) What ye might do when me back is turned, is a thing I would know nothing at all about.

(*All resume their drinks, which are nearly full, the* SERGEANT *standing very aloof with his back to the counter. He appears to be engrossed in his notebook.*)

PETER We might as well be hung for sheep as lambs, I suppose.

MR C. (*dismally*) Yes, indeed. We all know you have the terrible time of it, Sergeant, in the performance of your duty.

PETER (*moves to bar*) Begob and you're right, Mr Coulahan.

MR C. It would be as much as my livelihood or your promotion in the force was worth for me to offer you a drink after hours in these premises. Or for you to accept it—even on such a blasted, blizzardy one like this when the flesh might be skinned off your bones and you in the pursuit of your duty. Think of that, gentlemen!

PETER It's tough, right enough, Sergeant. (*He turns to* SERGEANT.)

MR C. If I was caught offering you a drink after hours, Sergeant, I could be brought up on the gravest charges— bribery, corruption and attempted suborning of the police force.

(JEM *moves to bar.*)

JEM God save us, Mr Coulahan!

MR C. What would happen to you, Sergeant, I don't rightly know at all—not being fully acquainted with the rules, regulations and disciplinary measures governing the Civic Guards or Gawrdah Sheekawnah, as now known. (*Sighs deeply.*) We both have the hard times of it, Sergeant, and that's the truth. (*He turns for bottles behind him.*) A strong ball of malt is what I'm badly in need of myself at this moment—what with being perished with the cold all day. (*Pours drink.*) And now, at night, with a breach of closed hours on me hands. (*Sighs heavily and takes drink.*)

JEM True enough. The cold was somethin' fierce today. Desperate. You'd want mufflers round yer legs as well as round yer neck.

PETER Well, the summer won't be long now.

COULAHAN The summer? (*Sighs.*) D'you remember last August, Sergeant?

SERGEANT I do and I don't, Mr Coulahan. I do and I don't.

MR C. It was the grand month of summer weather, Sergeant. I was out swimming twice. The water was like soup. And begob the heat of the rocks would nearly burn the feet off you.

JEM I never fancied the water at all, Mr Coulahan. Never had any time for it. It's not a natural thing to be getting into. It's alright for fish, of course.

MR C. That month of August was so hot it—it put me in mind of the First War—when I was out beyond in Messpott!

JEM Holy God, where's that?

MR C. Messiopotamia! Did ye never hear tell of Messiopotamia? And there was me fighting the Turks and the Arabs—fighting for small nationalities! That's the quare one, Sergeant. That month of summer we had brought me back to the First World War.

SERGEANT Them two Great Wars were desperate and ferocious encounters.

PETER I suppose it was very hot out there?

MR C. Hot did you say? I don't believe there was heat anywhere like it before or after. It was a class of heat that people in this part of the world wouldn't understand at all. Forty years ago and more and I can still feel that sun beyond in Shatt-el-Arab. That was where we landed.

(*The* SERGEANT *takes no notice and* MR C. *quietly refills his own drink and pulls three stouts, the third of which he places on the counter between himself and the* SERGEANT.)

PETER Was there—much sunstroke?

MR C. Sunstroke? We thought the heat in the ship was bad enough—and so it was—till we landed! Nearly three thousand of us! (*Gasps.*) The first thing I feels walking down the gangway is a big rush of hot air up me nose. The heat was beltin' up outa the ground like smoke out of an engine. The air was so thin and so hot that you wouldn't feel yourself breathing it. It was—stretched out, d'you know. Thinned out be the heat coming at it outa the ground and outa the sky and all sides. It was dried and no moisture in it at all—like a withered pea. (*Pause.*) It was like putting your head into an oven and taking a deep breath.

PETER I wouldn't fancy that at all—bad as the weather is in Ireland, it's better than that.

MR C. You haven't heard the half, so you haven't. We weren't finished gasping for breath, when another desperate thing happened! The lads were hours coming off the boat, and the rest of us was lined up there on the quayside. It was this way—I got tired standing on me feet—if you know what I mean—and went to change me weight from one foot to the other. Well, do you know what I'm going to tell you? My feet was stuck. (*They gasp.*) Stuck to the ground.

JEM Begob, ye musta had spikes in them.

MR C. Spikes be damned! Weren't we all standing there in our tropical rubber-soled shoes, and wasn't all the rubber melting under us.

JEM I never heard the like of that. Never.

MR C. A thousand men lined up there on the quay—and not one of them able to budge. My God, it was fierce! Fierce!

JEM Did you ever throw a bit of rubber inta the fire by accident? Begob, the hum off it would destroy yer nose altogether.

MR C. Of course, we were soldiers. No question of 'Please, Sir, I'm stuck to the ground, Sir! Me shoes is meltin', Sir, what'll I do, Sir?' None of that class of thing at all. Oh, no. It was just a question of standing there, waiting for the order to quick march. You shoulda seen us when we got the order. D'you know what it was like? Did you ever see a fly—a fly trying to walk off a fly-paper?

JEM I know what you mean—exactly! Buzzin' and roarin' and twistin' and workin' away with the legs—up to his neck in sticky stuff.

MR C. Just like flies on a fly-paper we were.

JEM Isn't that I was sayin'?

MR C. It was a march of only two hundred yards to our quarters—but it was the dirtiest—sweatiest—stickiest—and driest march we ever had. Every man in a lather of sweat, his clothes stickin' to his skin, and his tongue hangin' outa him lika dog's.

(*Here both* JEM *and* PETER *take long and resounding slugs from their cool drinks. The* SERGEANT *fusses uncomfortably with his book as if determined to take no interest in* MR C.'*s recital.*)

PETER Begob, Sergeant, and me own tongue's beginnin' to hang out like a dog's as well!

MR C. Well, begging the Sergeant's pardon and kind indulgences, I'm going to have a ball of malt meself because I feel the want of it after thinking about me days as a soldier out in Messpot, God help me. (COULAHAN *drinks.*)

SERGEANT (*ponderously*) I'm finishing up me notes here—and when me notes is finished, we'll all have to say good night and go home to our beds—and thank God we have beds to go to.

JEM You never spoke a truer word, Sergeant. Sometimes I do be . . .

SERGEANT There might be murders and all classes of illegalities goin' on behind me back, but what I don't see I don't know . . .

JEM That's a fact, Sergeant.

SERGEANT The Law is a very—intricate thing. And nobody knows it better than meself.

MR C. Spoken like a sensible man, Sergeant, and we're all very grateful. We know you're only doin' your duty. Just the same as we were when we were servin' in the King's uniform out in Messiopotamia before it was burnt off our backs with the heat.

PETER I suppose you had many a bad time after the day you landed in the rubber shoes?

MR C. Bad times? BAD TIMES did ye say? Did I not . . . (*Gulps another drink.*) Did I not tell you about the desert?

JEM You did not. (*Pause.*)

MR C. We had some desperate times out in the desert. No man that lived through that will ever have the memory of it off his mind—not even if he had his brain washed—and that's a fact!

JEM Begob, and I'd hate to have me brain washed! It's bad enough havin' yer . . .

MR C. There was a detachment of Arab madmen sighted away out in the desert near some oasis or other—There they were, musterin' together to get ready to come in and attack us . . .

PETER Begor . . .

MR C. Maybe there was a thousand of them in it, and others comin' in on camels to join them.

PETER I'd be nervous of camels.

MR C. So the order comes down that we're all to march out and go for them before they had a chance to get themselves into battle-order. (*Sips drink.*) That was the way it was. I'll never forget it—as long as I live—never! (*Pause.*)

PETER Were they far out in the desert?

MR C. I'd say—I'd say—about twenty-five or—mebbe thirty miles—as the crow flies.

JEM Does there be crows in the desert?

MR C. At six o'clock in the morning—sic ack-emma we called it—we got the order. (*In Sergeant-Major's voice.*) *Get ready to march in two hours.* (*Normal voice.*) On with the rubber shoes and the packs and the belts and the water-bottles, and the bloody big rifles! It was a load that would kill a man in his health. Then out on parade. (*Sergeant-Major voice.*) *Quick March! Left, right, left, right!* (*Normal voice.*) Away out into the wilds with us—a straggling string of men staggering out into the burning sand. (*He drinks.*) A twenty-four hours forced march. (*Puts down glass.*) But we were bet—bet to the ropes! It was the shoes again.

JEM Didn't I tell ye?

MR C. (*drinks again*) Then the rubber began to melt again—and give out little puffs of smoke. Soon the feet began to be roasted like two joints with a fire under them!

PETER The Lord save us!

MR C. Don't be talkin', man! When I'd got an extra stab of heat in the feet, I'd give a lep inta the air with the pain of it.

JEM I declare to me God!

MR C. But when I'd come down on the sand again, I'd get worse roastin' from the weight of the lep—showers of sparks flyin' right, left and centre. (*Drinks again.*) And d'you know what was happenin' all this time?

JEM I suppose the enemy lads was lyin' in wait behind the trees?

MR C. What trees?

JEM Wouldn't there be all classes of palm trees about the place?

MR C. Well, I'll tell you what was happenin' (*Drinks again.*) I declare to God the sun began to come down on top of us —outa the sky! Every minute that passed, it seemed to be lower—and lower—down—down—on top of our heads. The heat, gentlemen—the heat! (*Gulps hurriedly.*) I can nearly feel it still. Then after a while I felt a queer thing happenin'.

JEM I was goin' to say that.

PETER Would ye shut up, and let . . .

MR C. After a little while I begun to dry up!

PETER Dry up?

MR C. Every bit of me begun to get dried up and withered. The first thing that went outa order was the tongue and the mouth. Me tongue begun to get dry and cracked! And then it begun to get—bigger!

JEM Oh, Holy Hour!

♣ 111 ♣

MR C. It swelled out till it nearly choked me and got as hard and dry as a big cinder. I couldn't swally with it! (*All three gulp drinks.*) The whole inside of me mouth got dry and cracked the same way—and so did me neck and all inside me.

PETER The Lord between us and all harm!

MR C. It was like bein' grilled—except there was no gravy.

PETER I suppose the eyes were affected, too.

MR C. Don't be talkin' man! The eyes—the eyes begun to get singed and burnt at the edges. And, as well as that, the watery part dried up in a way that was something fierce. (*Pause.*) Before I know where I was—the eyebrows were gone!

PETER No!

MR C. Withered and scorched away be the heat they were— Hell itself. (*Gulps another drink.*) It was terrible. There we were, staggerin' through the bloody—brazen—boilin'— blanketty-blank heat. The skin chippin' and curlin' off our faces. Our bodies dryin' up and witherin' into wrinkles like —prunes! And the worst of it—a hot, dry thirst comin' up outa our necks, like the blast from a furnace. Oh, my God, it was desperate—desperate. (*He gulps again.*) D'you know the first thing the lads done—nearly every one of them? (*Pause.*) Took off their water-bottles—and threw them away. And do you know why? Do you know why? (*Pause.*) I'll tell you why—the water-bottles were made of metal. Some class of anumilliyum—anumilliyum as thin as paper. When that sun got to work on them bottles, I needn't tell you what happened. First of all, the water got up near to boiling-point. Even if you could hold the bottle in your hand and open it, the water would be no good to you—because it would scald the neck off you. There was only one thing to do with the bottles—get rid of them! Matteradam what else happens.

PETER Wasn't it terrible, throwin' away bottles full of water in the middle of the desert.

MR C. Well, there you are—there you are.

JEM Of course you coulda buried all the bottles deep down in a hole and come back for them when the thirst was at you. The water'd be nice and cool then.

PETER And what happened after that?

MR C. What happened after that is not a thing I would like to swear to because—the heat began to have a very bad effect —up here—(*Tapping forehead.*)—in the attic.

PETER I suppose so.

MR C. There's a lot of moisture and blood and so on in the brain, y'know. The brain is like a wet sponge, and very queer things are goin' to happen. Very queer things.

PETER I suppose you're lucky to be alive at all.

MR C. Very queer things. (*Lowering voice.*) The first thing was—I lost me sense of direction! I didn't know whether me head was me heels or whether I was standin' or sittin', d'you know? I was fallin' all over the place.

PETER I declare to me——

MR C. So were the other lads—walkin' and crawlin' on top of each other—every man as dry as a brick, with his tongue swollen out in his parched mouth half-chokin' him. And— the—thirst!!! My God, the thirst!!!!

(SERGEANT *comes to counter and takes three drinks, one by one, and drinks them.*)

SERGEANT Tell me, lads. Tell me—does anybody mind if I sing 'The Rose of Tralee'?

(*They all sing.*)

Faustus Kelly

by
Myles na gCopaleen

FAUSTUS KELLY was first produced at the Abbey Theatre, Dublin, on the 25th January, 1943, with the following players: KELLY, *F. J. McCormick*; CULLEN, *Fred Johnston*; REILLY, *Michael J. Dolan*; KILSHAUGHRAUN, *Brian O'Higgins*; HOOP, *Denis O'Dea*; TOWN CLERK, *Cyril Cusack*; MRS CROCKETT, *Ria Mooney*; HANNAH, *Eileen Crowe*; CAPTAIN SHAW, *Gerard Healy*; and MR STRANGE, *Liam Redmond*. It was produced by *Frank Dermody* with settings by *Michael Clarke*.

Characters in the play

KELLY	*Chairman of the Urban Council*
CULLEN REILLY HOOP	*Members of the Council*
SHAWN KILSHAUGHRAUN	*An ex-T.D., also a member*
TOWN CLERK	*A Corkman*
MRS MARGARET CROCKETT	*A widow*
HANNAH	*Her maid*
CAPTAIN SHAW	*A visitor*
THE STRANGER	*?*

Prologue

Stage is blacked out. A faint white light picks out the head and shoulders of the Devil and the head of KELLY. *The Devil is standing behind* KELLY, *who is seated signing a diabolical bond. When he has it signed, the Devil reaches out a green-tinted claw and snatches up the document with a sharp rustling noise. Immediately there is a complete black-out.*

Act 1

The setting of the First Act is the Council Chamber, which is also used by the Town Clerk as his office. It is a spacious room with a window at side, left; the door is left. The TOWN CLERK'S *desk with adjacent typist's table and various office effects are on the right-hand side of the room. In the remaining two-thirds of the floor space stand the large table and chairs used for meetings of the Council. The side of the table faces audience and one side should be long enough to accommodate four chairs.* REILLY *and* KILSHAUGHRAUN *sit at the ends in Act I. At back is a recessed platform railed off and marked with a sign* 'SILENCE: *Public Gallery.' When the curtain goes up* CULLEN *and* REILLY *are discovered in casual attitudes, evidently waiting for the others.*

CULLEN That was a bad business out the road, Martin.

REILLY I was just saying today that if we didn't do something to control them motorcars, they'll wipe out the whole lot of us.

CULLEN I wouldn't blame the motorcar, Martin. The motorcar is man's friend. Fair is fair. Blame where blame is due, as the man said. Where do you leave Mister John Barleycorn?

REILLY O, I know. I'm not making any excuse for that, the driver was fluthered, I'm told. And the lady was no better. A very bold article, I believe, with a man's breeches on her—

CULLEN Well, there you are! A young drunken pup flying around the country in transports of intoxication, killing hens, cows, pigs and Christians—*and you blame the motorcar!* What sort of reasoning is that, man?

REILLY (*with great feeling*) I'd like to see all the motorcars in the world destroyed.

CULLEN Faith, Martin, I often think you're not all in it.

REILLY I'm sure of one thing—it's only in a motorcar you'd see a bold article like her with her trousers and her brazen face and her big backside.

CULLEN (*laughing*) Ah, Martin, you're very hard on the poor motorcars.

REILLY (*paying no attention*) Isn't it a terrible thing to have young people misbehavin' and drivin' around drunk and killin' people? Is it any wonder they have them retreats above in the Chapel?

CULLEN Maybe they were brother and sister.

REILLY And what brother, in God's name, would let his sister go around with pants on?

CULLEN (*doubtfully*) O, I don't know. (*Reflectively.*) My own sister Maggie, now, or a girl with that class of a figure . . .

REILLY (*exploding*) Get away outa that, man, for pity's sake. You ought to be ashamed of yourself . . . (*Gets up and looks out of window. Comes back frowning.*) There's nothing but trousers in Russia, I'm told. Men, women and children go about all day working at ingines and thrashing machines, no privacy or home-life or respect for womanhood. That's where *you* ought to be, in Russia. Away out with a crowd of madmen thrashing and working away for further orders. Father Peter was telling me that a business like that can't last. Couldn't possibly last.

CULLEN (*smiling some good-humour back into the conversation*) Russia, is it? Ah, a beautiful but distant land. The Russian bear, the Russian steamroller. The Volga, the Vistula and the Dnieper. The grave of Napoleon's Grand Army. Never fear, Martin, ould Ireland's good enough for me. (*He pauses.*) The Big Man, Mr Kelly, is late tonight. So are the others.

REILLY The Chairman's late every night but always in time to bawl off some unfortunate man that's two minutes later.
(*He sits.*)

CULLEN True enough. Do you remember the night he went for me? (*Mimicking.*) *Am I to understand, Mr Cullen, that you desire to have your name recorded as having been present at this meeting?* Don't exert yourself talking, Mr Chairman, says I, till you get your breath back, because them stairs would kill a horse! (*Laughs appreciatively.*) Wasn't it good? He was just in before me. 'Don't exert yourself talking Mr Chairman, till you get your breath back because them stairs would kill a horse.'

REILLY (*very drily*) Yes.

CULLEN I think I hear the bould Shawn.

REILLY (*makes a grimace of distaste and rises stiffly and shambles to the window*) Well, for God's sake keep him off politics because that fellow has me worn out with his politics.

CULLEN Good evening to you, Shawn.

(SHAWN KILSHAUGHRAUN *enters from main door, back right. He is a thick, smug, oafish character, dressed in a gawkish blue suit. He exudes a treacly good-humour, always wears an inane smile and talks with a thick*

♣ 121 ♣

western brogue upon which sea-weed could be hung. Hangs hat on stand, right of door.)

SHAWN Bail o Dhia annso isteach. Hullo, Tom. And how is Martin.

REILLY (*sourly*) Martin is all right.

SHAWN (*expansively*) Well, isn't it the fine glorious Summer evening, thanks be to God. Do you know, the air is like wine. I'm half drunk, drinkin' it in. Ah, but 'tis grand. A walk on a day like that would do you as much good as a good iron tonic.

CULLEN It's great weather, there's no doubt. I'd like to take off all my clothes and lie out in the meadow as stark naked as God made me.

REILLY (*turning quickly from the window*) You'd get all you want of that carry-on in Russia. You can wheel a wheelbarra down the main street of Moscow without a stitch on you and the people will say you've a nice new barra. That's the place for you—Russia. (*Sits right of table.*) He's off to Russia, Shawn, that's the latest.

SHAWN Do you tell me so?

REILLY He's going to make his sister, Maggie, wear trousers and drive a thrashing-mill. If he could find a mine, he'd send me and you down, to be working with pneumatic artillery in the bowels of the earth and blasting tons of rocks and stuff down on top of us. Two miles down he'd send us.

SHAWN Yerrah, now, you're coddin' me surely. You're trying to take a rise out of me. (*Sits left of table.*)

CULLEN Don't mind him, Shawn.

SHAWN But who would see him if he was stretched in his natural state in the meadow? Sure the grass is up to here, look, and lovely rich juicy Irish grass it is.

CULLEN Certainly.

SHAWN Sure if you drove a small motorcar into *my* meadow in the morning, you wouldn't know where to look for it in

the evening. (*Caressingly.*) Lovely, tall, nourishing, splendid grass, food and drink for any taste. And nice fresh crisp
hay it will make, gorgeous golden hay. You won't find
anything like it outside Ireland.

REILLY What about the Czar's grass beyond in Russia?

CULLEN Ah, sure the ould Czar went to the wall years ago.
Years ago, man.

SHAWN As a young man, the Russian Revolution was a
thing that fired me imagination.

REILLY If you ask me, them Russians would ate any hay you
gave them. Damn the one of them ever heard of a good
plate of bacon and cabbage. Vodka and beans is all the
order there, I believe. How would you fancy that after ten
hours on the thrashing-machine?

SHAWN A man was once telling me that in Russia they do
have the new potatoes in March. I daresay it's due to the
Gulf Stream. Imagine a plate of new spuds on St Patrick's
Day. They'd have the new peas, too. (*With feeling.*)
Begorrah, I'd spend ten years on a thrashing-machine for
that.

CULLEN (*at the window*) I think I see a certain Town Clerk
wending his weary way.

SHAWN I believe that man Stalin is a black Protestant.

REILLY He looks like an Orangeman to me.

CULLEN Here he is. (*Mimics Cork accent.*) *Good ev'nin'. How
are ye's at all? Is de Big Man not here?* Shhhhhh!
(*The* TOWN CLERK *enters. He is a small perky man of
about* 30, *wears the fáinne and is well dressed. He has a
strong Cork accent.*)

TOWN CLERK Good ev'nin'. How are ye's at all. Isn't it very
warm? Is de Big Man not here? (*He goes to desk left.*)

REILLY Mr Kelly is having a few rossiners down the way
and will be here when the temperature below his belt has
risen to the right pitch.

TOWN CLERK (*taking papers from desk and going to table*) I was thinking of going up to Dublin tomorrow, please God, to see the Minister's Private Secretary. He's a personal friend of me married sister and he's half-Cork on the da's side . . . He's a right dacent man, I met him wan time at the Metropole Hotel in Cork and we got on together . . . (*he looks up*) like two canaries in a cage.

SHAWN You're roight, me bucko. A soft . . . . well-made . . . dacent . . . God-fearing . . . Irish gentleman.

TOWN CLERK Yerrah, don't be talking to me. I was inside in the hotel with Paddy Hourigan, the Lord have mercy on him, an didn't we run into the Minister's Secretary on the stairs.

SHAWN Ah, Paddy Hourigan, may God be good to him, for a finer, neater, better-made, dacenter Irishman never wore a hat.

TOWN CLERK Yerrah, don't be talking to me. 'Meet Mr Hinnissey,' says Paddy. (*He faces the company.*) 'I don't know Mr Hinnissey,' says the Minister's Secretary, 'but I've heard all about him.' 'Come into the bar,' says he to me, 'and have a glawsheen.'

REILLY And I suppose you walked in and drank the pockets off him.

TOWN CLERK Now, Martin, now, now——

REILLY You're another man that ought to go to Russia.

TOWN CLERK Russia?

REILLY Begob, they'd know how to handle you there, me boyo. They don't believe in letting able-bodied young fellas live like leeches on the backs of the ratepayers there —no bloody fear. You'll work for your money there, not heating the seat of a stool but out drivin' ingines with the sweat and the muck plastered on you.

TOWN CLERK I'll go tomorrow if the Council pays me fare.

REILLY (*angrily, his voice rising*) By God, they'd make a man of *you*, then, if they had you out there. Damn the Russian ratepayer *you'd* live on. You wouldn't get away with this four fifty a year stuff, with fees for fairs and markets.

TOWN CLERK (*laughs as he sits, going through files*) Ah, dear-a-dear.

SHAWN (*seriously*) Tell me, Martin. Phwat are the rates in Russia at the present time?

REILLY The rates?

SHAWN Ay, the rates.

REILLY (*puzzled*) Well I don't know the figures but I know this—the unfortunate rate-payers out there aren't saddled with thruppence in the pound for teaching Irish and filling the heads of a lot of poor chisellers with 'taw may go h-mahs' and 'Gurramahaguts' and the Lord knows what bogman's back-chat.

TOWN CLERK Ah, ná bí ag cainnt!

REILLY You shut your Cork gob and keep it shut!

SHAWN Now isn't it a terrible ting to see two fine grand Irishmen fighting and back-biting one another to their faces? Isn't it a great shame to see ye playing England's game in the offices of the Urban District Council?

CULLEN (*going back to table and sitting*) I suppose it's true that Kelly's going up at the by-election.

REILLY O, it's true enough. My God, imagine that bags a T.D.!

SHAWN I do, I do. The Chairman is going to stand. 'Tis great trouble and tribulation, a T.D.'s life. 'Tis no life for an idealist.

TOWN CLERK Do you know, Shawn, there's wan thing that often puzzled me, many's a time I meant to ask you about it. How did you come to lose your seat at all, at all?

SHAWN I'll tell you, boy. Instid . . . of getting work on the roads for strong farmers . . . and instid of getting young farmers' sons into the Electricity Supply Board . . . and instid of gitting the old age pinshin for men with big fortunes that weren't the age . . . phwat was I at only planting little fir trees on the mountains that I love above meself.

CULLEN Tell me, Shawn, have you got the time for God's sake? What time is it by your gold watch and chain?

SHAWN (*takes out large metal watch*) I do, I do. The correct time according to me wireless is ten minutes past nine.

TOWN CLERK Mr Kelly must have been delayed on the road. I want to have a private conversation with him about me visit to Dublin.

REILLY Ten to one you're off to Dublin to work some election twist for Kelly.

TOWN CLERK De Chairman's all in favour of keeping de Minister on our hands. The two is personal friends, I believe. Did you get any offer for that small farm o' yours, Shawn? The one out de Lochatubber road?

SHAWN I do. A man rang me up on the wire about it four days ago offering four hundred pounds. Well, do you know, I took him to task. Listen to me here, man, says I, do you know that the man you are talking to is Shawn Kilshaughraun? Do you take me, says I, for a gawm from Kirry or some hungry remote cold distant townland in the County Cork?

REILLY Maybe he knew his man. By God, I wouldn't fancy doing business with you.

TOWN CLERK Now, Martin. (*He puts a finger to his lips.*) You've had yer say. Hould yer whisht for pity's sake.
(*He walks to desk and takes large ledgers, brings them to his table and works at them.*)

SHAWN Sure he hadn't a word to say when I was finished talking to him. Don't you know, says I, that the soil of me little farm is (*caressingly*) the grandest, finest, richest fertile land in de whole country. I was talking to an Inspector from the Department about the soil. Mr Kilshaughraun, says he, you'll be surprised at what I'm goin' to tell ye.

CULLEN What did he say?

SHAWN Do you know, says he, that in all me travels I have nivir come across soil the like of this. It has phosphates, says he, and the divil knows what. I disremember the names of all the fine, grand, nourishing, rich, juicy properties of me soil. Sure Lord save us, haven't I a field of oats up there now, as yellow as a bantam's tail, as thick as a girl's hair, sure you'd nivir find yer way out if you walked into it.

REILLY Sure don't I pass it every Sunday on me walk after Mass, a rough-lookin' hungry farm of rocks and scraws that would wear the hands off five men to get any satisfaction out of it in a month of Sundays. Sure don't I know it well. Six pound valuation on land, four on buildings. (*Bitterly.*) Ask the Town Clerk. Sure it's down on the list.

TOWN CLERK Dat's right, dat's right.

REILLY Ask the Chief Executive Officer of the Urban Council, four fifty a year with fees for fairs and markets for the privilege of sitting on his Cork backside! Do you know, I think I'm going off me head in this place . . . What in the name of God is keepin' that Chairman? I've a good mind to go home and leave him without his quorum.

CULLEN Yerra, take your time, Martin. Sure what would you be doin' at home only annoying Mrs Reilly, yer good long-suffering wife, with your great unrest of mind.

TOWN CLERK (*working at his books*) Well, do you know, these books are in a terrible condition of confusion. Full of blanks. Do 'oo know phwat the Council was paid four years ago for 27 planks that were sold to de County Surveyor?

SHAWN (*expansively*) A good strong well-made, well-seasoned plank of prime timber is worth twelve shillings and sixpence.

TOWN CLERK (*tapping his ledger*) Blank! That's what was paid—Blank!

(*He rises again and goes to desk to get papers.*)

REILLY Of course, the poor man that was here before you had the great misfortune to be born in this town. He was not a smart maneen from Cork with his degrees and all his orders, he was only paid four pounds a week and fees for markets turned in to the Council, (*his voice rises*) he was only an ordinary unassuming decent Irishman that took a bottle of stout like the rest of us, with no flying up to Dublin to the Departments to suck up to a lot of thumawns and polthogues and fly-be-nights . . .

(*Quite suddenly the door is opened by* KELLY. *He is accompanied by* THE STRANGER—*a small dark middle-aged man who is formally dressed in striped trousers, black coat and wears a bowler hat. He carries a brief-case. He is motioned into the public gallery at the back of the stage and throughout the Act he sits immovably with his hat on, facing the audience. He receives many curious looks from those present.* MR KELLY *is dressed in a black overcoat, dark scarf and hard hat. He wears glasses, has a cunning, serious face. In his left hand he carries dark leather gloves. He has taken the company completely by surprise. They preserve a complete and surprised silence, which* KELLY *naturally takes as a tribute to his own great importance. The others seem to be asking themselves whether he has been listening outside the door for a time before coming in.* SHAWN *says* 'Hullo'. KELLY *closes the door with great care. He then takes his overcoat off slowly, hangs it up, puts his hat on the same peg and comes forward to the table slowly and abstractedly, his gaze being downwards and meeting nobody's eye. He then looks up with a mechanical smile.)*

KELLY Good evening, gentlemen. Good evening, Town Clerk. A pleasant summer evening, thank God. How is your good lady, Martin? I believe she had a touch of cold.

REILLY (*non-committally*) Mrs Reilly is all right, thank ye.

KELLY Ah, good. Shawn, I want a word with you afterwards at your convenience. (*He rubs his hands together briskly.*)

SHAWN I do, I do. With pleasure, Chairman.

CHAIRMAN I want you to see the Minister about a certain matter. A word in the right place, you know. A little matter I want set right. There is certain backstairs work going on about the Fair Green, cattle-jobbers and publicans butting at one another to get the site changed, first here and then there. Result: delay, delay, delay. No Fair Green and the streets up to your ankles in it of a fair day. (*He realises that he still has his gloves in his hand: sighs.*) But that's another matter. It's not on the Agenda.

(*He turns and walks back to his coat to leave his gloves.*)

SHAWN I endorse, and I re-endorse, every word you say, Chairman. The streets, of a fair day, are a crying, desperate, insanitary shame. Isn't it a terrible thing to have publicans putting down money to have the Fair held at their doors? Wouldn't it make you disheartened in democracy? Wouldn't it now?

(KELLY *returns to the table, sits down carefully in the large chair at the head of it, sighs and smiles indulgently.*)

KELLY Human nature, Shawn, not democracy. Poor old human nature.

CULLEN It doesn't matter where you hold the Fair, you'll have to drive the animals there and back and how are you going to make them behave themselves?

TOWN CLERK (*moving over to the Chairman's left with a heap of ledgers*) I was just saying, Chairman, that I'm off to Dublin some of these fine days to the Department about a certain ting. The personal touch is a very important thing, you know.

REILLY 'Touch' is right. Up to Dublin on the ratepayers' money to bum drinks off the highest in the land and to work some electioneering twist.

KELLY Gentlemen, we must have some order, some system, a little mutual respect. The Town Clerk will go to Dublin when he is instructed to do so by the Council. In the meantime, Mr Reilly, he is entitled to the respect that is due to his office——

REILLY Ah, yerra——

KELLY —as Chief Executive Officer of this town. The dignity of the town is represented in his person.

REILLY (*sarcastically*) I see.

SHAWN Just as a Minister or a deputy is entitled to the respect that is due to the sovereign people of Ireland. Do you understand me, Martin? The Irish nation. (*He begins to pick his teeth.*)

CULLEN I don't see anything wrong with the Town Clerk, and Cork isn't the worst place to come from. Didn't Foley the sculptor come from Cork.

REILLY Who?

CULLEN Foley.

REILLY I suppose *he* died for Ireland, too.

KELLY (*rapping the table gently with his spectacle-case*) Now, gentlemen, order, ORDER. A little bit of order, now. Mr Kilshaughraun, I would like your attention, please.

SHAWN (*desisting from picking his teeth abstractedly*) I do, I do, Mr Chairman, I do, I do.

KELLY And yours, Mr Cullen. Mr Reilly, too. I have a

meeting with the P.P. at nine and we will want to proceed with expedition . . . and despatch so that I may get away in time. A little matter of the Christmas Coal Fund, very trivial but very important to the unfortunate poor of this town. Now, Town Clerk.

TOWN CLERK (*in a toneless, official voice*) De following members are absent from this meeting, Mr P. Meady, Mr George Pealahan, Mrs Mary Corkey——

SHAWN (*with feeling*) Ah, the poor woman, the poor . . . suffering . . . patient . . . pious . . . decent, saintly . . . soul, she'll never lave that bed again. Sure I seen her——

TOWN CLERK (*raising his voice*) Mr J. D. Callen and Mr Joe Hoop.

CULLEN I agree with you, Shawn: Dr Dan says it's only a question of time. Decent woman, too. (JOE HOOP *enters*.) O, here's Joe. Good night Joe, you're just in time.

HOOP (*in a pronounced northern accent and giving a broad smile*) Good night.

> (*He is a tall, youngish man, hatless and coatless, wears glasses and is of somewhat studious aspect. He carries what appears to be a novel in his hand. He slumps into his chair, opens the book, which he holds half under the table, and begins to read it. He pays no attention whatever to the meeting, reading his book steadily to the end. He sits right of table between* REILLY *and* CULLEN.)

TOWN CLERK (*speaking in a toneless headlong babble*) The Minutes of the last meeting. Letter from the Department was read in connection with the Council's housing scheme: letter was noted. Letter from the Commissioners of Public Works was read in connection with de preservation of de old clocktower in Hogan Street: ordered dat de Council view dis proposal with approval and Town Clerk to co-operate with de Commissioners to de best of his ability, no charge to fall upon de rates from his preservation proposal.

Letter read from de Department in connection with de Council's share in next year's allocation under de Free Milk Scheme: ordered dat de Council press for high allocation in view of large number of expectant mothers now on de rates and de depressed state of de town ginerally. (*His voice tails off as a conversation begins.*)

CULLEN Tell me, Chairman. Is it true you're going up at the by-election?

KELLY That is a big question, Mr Cullen.

REILLY If you're not, it won't be for want of having a high opinion of yourself, anyway.

CULLEN It's all over the town that you're going up.

KELLY Gentlemen, I am not yet quite certain where my duty lies. My desire is to serve. Whether I can best serve by offering myself as a candidate for the national parliament is a matter for consideration.

REILLY (*impatiently*) Are you going up? Yes or no? Cut out the blather.

KELLY This much I *will* say. I have been *pressed* to go forward. Certain friends are very insistent. Certain friends will not take 'no'. I may have to stand eventually to satisfy them. I only wish I was as worthy as their opinion of me would indicate.

REILLY It must be terrible to be pushed like that against your will.

CULLEN Well, more luck to you if you do decide to stand. You'll get two votes from my house, anyway.

KELLY Thank you, Mr Cullen.

REILLY Begob, if you ask me, this bloody country's on its last legs. With you in parliament it'll be the limit altogether.

KELLY I'm not in parliament yet, Mr Reilly. Let us cross that bridge when we come to it. Proceed, Town Clerk.

TOWN CLERK Letter read from Miss Peake, typist, asking

de Council for increase of 5/- a week in her salary: ordered dat de increase be given in view of Miss Peake's valuable services to de Council and de Community, subject to de sanction of de Minister for Local Government and Public Health and Department to be informed dat Miss Peake has five years' unblemished service in which she discharged her duties with great zeal and efficiency to de satisfaction of de Council and de Town Clerk and dat she worked late on several occasions in de office of de Town Surveyor when he was getting his works into order and dat she is a very good girl in every way. Letter read from de Department inquiring what action de Council took on Circular Letter of 10th May in connection with de cleaning of burial ground: ordered dat de Department be informed dat de grave-yard is in a first-class condition and always has been and dat no action be taken on de Circular. De Council discussed de disgraceful condition of de footpath in Emmet Street near de Chairman's house. Chairman said dat de place was a menace to life and limb of a dark night and dat de road contractor be warned to put the road into proper repair de way he found it and dat de Town Surveyor be ordered to put up a new lamp at dis place, which is very dangerous to pedestrian and vehicular traffic of a dark night. (*Voice trails off.*)

CULLEN Do you know, I don't see any necessity for an election. There's no need for it.

REILLY You're right there. We're bad as we are, but there's no reason for getting ourselves into a worse mess.

CULLEN Because what have they to do only get together, sink their differences and form a strong national government, a government that everybody in the land will respect?

KELLY Ah, Mr Cullen, if only poor old human nature could be mastered; if only we could re-mould the universe nearer to the heart's desire. I'm afraid poor old human nature is the trouble.

REILLY Don't deprive the poor Chairman of his chance, Tom.

CULLEN Why not, Mr Kelly?

KELLY I fear such a plan would not work, Mr Cullen.

(*Town Clerk, still at Minutes, mumbles something about filling of Rate Collectorship.*)

CULLEN But *why*, Mr Kelly?

KELLY Because between the parties, Mr Cullen, there is what we call . . . an ideological . . . antipathy.

REILLY A *what*?

KELLY Do I make myself clear, Mr Cullen?

CULLEN (*very doubtful*) Well . . . that's right, too . . . but still . . .

KELLY Oil and water, Mr Cullen.

CULLEN All the same, I don't see why they don't bury the hatchet and forget their differences and form a good strong national government composed of the best elements in the country. I mean—who wants an election?

REILLY The Chairman.

KELLY (*sternly*) What the Chairman wants, Mr Reilly, is a little order so that we may transact our business. The election is a constitutional requirement and must be accepted by all loyal citizens. (*He turns to Town Clerk and signs Minute Book. Then, briskly:*) Now, Town Clerk, what have we got on the Agenda?

TOWN CLERK (*briskly*) I've a few letters here, Chairman. Here's the usual one from the Tourist Association asking for the three guineas. We pay every year.

SHAWN (*nodding heavily*) I do, I do. Nivir was money better spent. We must do everything in our power to bring the beauties of this town that is so full of grand . . . historical . . . rich . . . archaeological and scenic wonders to the notice of the world at large—and to the notice of our own grand flesh and blood beyond the seas, the sea-divided Gael in America. Not three guineas I'd give them but four.

REILLY I never seen an American in this town in me life bar lads that come with Duffy's Circus.

CULLEN Ah, sure we might as well pay. It won't break us.

KELLY I think we are agreed that the subscription should be renewed. It would be a very retrograde step to cancel it. Results in such cases must be slow.

TOWN CLERK (*repeating slowly what he is writing*) 'Ordered . . . dat . . . de subscription . . . be . . . renewed.' (*Proceeds*) I've a letter here again from lad Shandon about de Small Dwellings loan. It's not a nice letter at all. He's very sharp. He talks about gombeen men. Will I read it for ye?

KELLY (*annoyed*) No. Mark the letter 'read'.

REILLY I'll back up any ratepayer but not that tinker's son. Tell him to go and have a jump for himself.

KELLY (*fingering his watch*) Now, Town Clerk, what else have we?

TOWN CLERK I've another letter from de Department here about Miss Peake de typist. (*He lifts his head from his papers.*) Begorrah, do 'oo know, they are very angry with us. (*He reads.*) 'De proposal cannot in any circumstances be entertained. This officer is on her present scale, 30 shillings by 5 to 45 shillings, for only one year and it is considered that this represents adequate remuneration having regard to de extent of her duties.'

REILLY (*angrily*) I suppose what *we* think doesn't matter.

SHAWN Ah, you know, the Government machine is a very slow . . . sure . . . finely-tempered instrument. They do have to refuse everything to be on the safe side.

REILLY (*ignoring Shawn, his voice rising*) I suppose the chosen and elected representatives of the people don't matter at all. They're just something for some jackeen in a Dublin back-office to kick around.

KELLY (*in mild deprecation*) Now, Mr Reilly, where will that get us?

CULLEN (*innocently*) It's a shame, because Miss Peake is a nice good little girl. A cousin of your own, Martin, I believe? A fine girl, God bless her.

REILLY And what are you yapping about? What about it if she *is* a cousin of mine? Doesn't she earn her hard-earned salary?

CULLEN Lord, I never said a word against her.

TOWN CLERK Of course, de increase would have to come out of de rates.

REILLY (*exploding*) What are *you* bleating and blathering about, you Cork fly-be-night, bleeding and besting the ratepayers to the tune of four hundred and fifty pounds a year with your fine fat fees for fairs and markets, too bloody cute to take a bottle of stout but up to Dublin on the bum on the two train every Saturday?

KELLY Order, Mr Reilly, please. ORDER!

REILLY I don't give a damn for you, the Minister or anybody else. (*He snaps his fingers.*) I don't give that for you.

SHAWN Yerra, now, we'll put de increase up agin.

KELLY I propose that we ask the Minister to reconsider the matter, Mr Kilshaughraun, to kindly interest himself in the matter on behalf of the Council. Is that agreed?
(REILLY, CULLEN *and* SHAWN *relax.*)

TOWN CLERK (*recording the decision*) Carried unanimously. *Nem. con.*, as the man said.

KELLY (*briskly*) Well, next business, please.

TOWN CLERK De next item is de election of a rate collector for de Number Two district. (*Sensation.*)

REILLY (*astonished*) WHAT!

CULLEN (*seriously, very surprised*) What's this, in the name of God? How could that be? How in God's name could that be, Town Clerk?

REILLY (*in a steady, cold voice*) You're a bloody Cork liar.

KELLY (*with firm but unemphatic precision*) Gentlemen, I am informed by the Town Clerk that the next business is the election of a rate collector. I am bound to consider it——

REILLY (*excited*) Be God, this sort of stuff won't work. You won't get away with this. There was no Notice of Motion. Ye can't fill a job without notice of motion——

KELLY As a matter of simple fact, Mr Reilly, there *was*. Let us have accuracy if nothing else.

CULLEN I don't understand this at all. I never heard a word about it.

REILLY There was no Notice of Motion. This is some class of a ready-up, and I'm not going to sit here and stand for it.

SHAWN I do, I do. There was Notice of Motion all right. I remimber it well. Handed in be the Chairman himself.

CULLEN It's the first I heard of it and that's the God's truth.

REILLY Be God, there's a ready-up here.

KELLY Town Clerk, was there notice of motion? Kindly acquaint the members with the facts of the situation.

REILLY (*roaring*) BE GOD, THERE'S A READY-UP HERE. There's a dirty crooked deal been put through here, if there isn't my name isn't Reilly. Some fly-be-night is being walked in on to the ratepayers' backs.

KELLY Town Clerk, will you please answer my inquiry and do so expeditiously?

TOWN CLERK (*searching among his records*) Notice of Motion was handed in by the Chairman in the following terms, that is to say (*pause*): 'I hereby give notice that I shall move at the next meeting of the Council that de vacancy for a rate collector in de Number Two district should be filled.' (*He looks up.*) Sealed, signed and delivered to me in person by the said Chairman. Sure it's all here in black and white in me book.

(KELLY *puts his head in his hands wearily.*)

REILLY (*excitedly*) Be Gob, you have it all off, haven't you?
It's down in your little book. (*The phone rings.*) It's down
in your little book!

TOWN CLERK (*rising to answer phone and ignoring Reilly*)
Excuse me now, gents.

REILLY (*almost shouting at Town Clerk, who has risen to
cross room to his own table where the phone is*) It's all down
in your bloody little book, you Cork twister.

KELLY Order, Order! Please control your language or I'll
leave the Chair.

TOWN CLERK (*on phone*) Hello, hello! Are you there?
Who's dat?

REILLY You'll leave the Chair? I dar you to leave the Chair.
I dar you and I double-dar you to leave the Chair——

TOWN CLERK (*shouting above Reilly's voice*) Hello!
HELLO! Who, Shawn? Shawn Kilshaughraun? He is.
He is indeed. Hold on to the wire now, avic! (*He turns to
the meeting.*) A call for yourself, Shawn, boy.

REILLY (*banging the table*) Because if you leave the Chair,
you won't be able to wheel your own man into this job (*his
voice rises*) and by the time the matter comes up again
there'll be a full quorum here—THAT'S WHY YOU
WON'T LEAVE THE CHAIR!

SHAWN (*loudly and unctuously on the phone*) I do, I do.
Shawn Kilshaughraun speaking.

REILLY THAT'S WHY YOU WON'T LEAVE THE
CHAIR!

CULLEN Ah, now there's too much bitterness in this room
tonight, God forgive us all.

KELLY At any rate there is far too much shouting and noise.
Nothing is the worse for being quietly said. We don't
shout when we are saying the most important thing we
ever say and that's our daily prayers. (SHAWN *on phone:
I do, I do.*) We are bound to consider everything on the

Agenda. We have no alternative. We must do everything in an orderly way, we must have some system. Notice of Motion first and then deal with the matter in due form and in proper time at the next meeting following. Order, a respect for the rules of civilised order, will enable us to do our work efficiently and promptly.

REILLY I SAY THAT'S WHY YOU WON'T LEAVE THE CHAIR! YOU'RE AFRAID OF YOUR BLOODY LIFE TO LEAVE THE CHAIR! YOU'RE AFRAID OF YOUR BLOODY LIFE TO LEAVE THE CHAIR!!

SHAWN (*from the phone*) I do, I do. Certainly. What's that? What? WHAT?

KELLY (*severely*) This much I will say, Mr Reilly. Your language is not only a reflection on yourself but an insult to Council and an affront to the people of this town. In offering abuse to my person as Chairman of this elective assembly, you offer it to your fellow townspeople. Having said that much, I will say no more. I will pass from that and ask the Council to deal with the matter which has been brought forward in due order by the Town Clerk. I refer to the filling of the vacancy in the Number Two district.

SHAWN (*on the phone*) She is, boy, A lovely ... mild ... grand ... good-natured article. I do, I do.

REILLY (*very quickly*) If you go ahead with this twist, well and good, but you'll rue the day, you'll rue the day—mind that. (*His voice rises.*) There was no Notice of Motion except what was cooked by that crooked Town Clerk. You must give notice under the Public Bodies Order. (*His voice rises to a shout and he bangs on the table.*) I take me stand on the Public Bodies Order.

(*He rises, kicks back his chair and stamps to the window, where he remains with his back to the audience: he turns his head and shouts:*)

I take me stand on the Public Bodies Order.

CULLEN Now, Martin, we have to go by what is written in the official Minute Book of the Clerk. If he says there was, that's an end to it.

TOWN CLERK Shure who would believe a Corkman?

SHAWN (*on the phone*) I do, I do.

KELLY Very well, gentlemen. I propose the appointment of a very excellent person who has always impressed those that know him with his modest and gentlemanly bearing. Though not a native of the town—indeed he is a stranger to it—he has come among us from larger and busier haunts of men—I refer to the capital city of our land—and given those of us who have the honour to partake of intimate social intercourse with him the benefit of an experience that is both wide and expressive of all that is best in contemporary affairs.

REILLY Lord save us! Lord save us!

KELLY A graduate of the National University which was founded by Cardinal Newman to enable the cream of our Catholic youth to partake of the benefits of University education, he read a distinguished course and gave every satisfaction to his masters. In the field of athletics he gave no mean account of himself, being to this day the possessor of a silver cup for the long jump. A member of the Gaelic League for ten years, he speaks the old tongue with a fluency that many a person twice his age might well envy. As straight as a rod in character, honest as the sun, courteous in all his dealings with his fellow men, I think he is the most suitable person we could hope for. I therefore propose formally that he be appointed by the Council. I think we are lucky and privileged to have him.

REILLY (*who has half-turned from the window to listen to this address with exaggerated signs of astonishment*) I wonder who this fellow is when he's at home. Begob there's wonderful people living in this town that I never met. He has the Irish, too, wha———? Taw shay mahogany! Kaykee will too!

SHAWN (*who has been listening intently at the phone suddenly bursts into a roar of rough laughing, which subsides into long gurgles with 'I do, I do' discernible here and there.*)

CULLEN Who is this, Mr Chairman? His name?

KELLY Oh, I beg your pardon. The gentleman's name is (*he hesitates and stammers in confusion*) ... Strange—Mr Strange.

SHAWN (*on the phone*) I do, I do, sure I could go down there any day on me bicycle, I could meet you in Biddie Brannigan's and have a glass of good Irish whiskey with you, what grander, finer thing could we do?

(REILLY, *who has left the window, walks right round the room and comes to rest facing down at the Chairman with his back three-quarters to the audience.*)

KELLY Mr Hoop, perhaps you would second my proposition. Perhaps you would be good enough.

HOOP (*looking up from his book*) Aye, surely.

TOWN CLERK (*reading what he is writing*) Seconded by Councillor Joseph Hoop.

REILLY (*still glaring down, speaking in a hard, subdued voice as if genuinely shocked*) I have seen many queer dirty jobs done in this room in me time but my God Almighty, I never thought I'd live to see this. Some fly-be-night that was never seen or heard of in this town, as sure as God a relation of the Chairman's or of that fancy widow Crockett that he's running after. WHO IS HE? Where is he from? Is he going to be wheeled in on to the ratepayers' backs just because he's related to the Chairman's fancy woman?

KELLY (*angrily, rising to his feet*) That's enough of that talk! I'll thank you to keep Mrs Crockett's name off your bad discourteous tongue.

REILLY (*excitedly*) Is that why? Eh! My God Almighty! (*He rounds on the others.*) Are yez going to stand for that? Eh!

KELLY This man is intoxicated!

TOWN CLERK He is a little bit inebriated with his own verbosity, if I may so remark.

CULLEN Martin, you're going too far. I always support the Chairman. He has never nominated a bad man yet. In any case the Minister will only sanction a man that is A1. I think we might give this man a trial. I don't know him personally.

REILLY (*in a low voice*) Tom, Tom, I'm ashamed of you. This man wants to get his own or this widow's relations in by the back door—(*he points*) look at the face of him, did you ever see shame plainly written on a man's face so plain!

KELLY May God forgive you, you ignorant and slanderous traducer of people who never hurt you.

SHAWN (*on phone*) He married a grand big heifer of a woman. I do, I do.

REILLY (*exploding*) Because I'm not going to stand for it, I'm not going to stay here in the same room with such criminality. (*He makes a mad rush for the coat-stand, grabs his hat, rushes to the door, wheels round and shouts a final denunciation*): We'll see, we'll see, whether you'll drive a coach and four through the Public Bodies Order. We'll see whether the Public Bodies Order is just a bit of paper! Wait and see, wait and see!

(*He slams the door and is gone. There is complete silence. KELLY mops his brow.*)

SHAWN (*on phone, very softly*) I do, I do, I do.

TOWN CLERK De proposal is passed, subject to de Minister's sanction. Begob, that's what you'd call a man that's very violent in himself, God be good to him.

KELLY (*philosophically*) This much I *will* say. As a younger man I was myself inclined to be a bit ... contumacious. A bit ... contumelious. Later I came to a realisation of the golden virtue of temperance. I do not refer to the subject of intoxicating drink. My allusion is rather to temperance of hand, act and tongue. For, after all, what is a gentleman but one who has his temper under perfect control? The exhibition we have witnessed is saddening. It was all very ... very ... sad. Let no man say, however, that I pass judgment. Nothing of the kind. Mr Reilly is a man for whom I have the highest regard. He has many golden qualities. He has his failings, too, one of them he displayed tonight. Gentlemen, I am very sorry.

(*The door is thrown open, interrupting the Chairman's address.* REILLY *rushes in bare-headed with a hat in his hand. He hurries to the stand, puts the hat on it, takes another one off it and jams it on his head. Then he rushes out again and slams the door, without a glance at the table.*)

More I will not say. Let us now pass from that and return to what is public rather than personal. Town Clerk, what is the next item?

TOWN CLERK (*jauntily slapping his book closed*) The next item, Mr Chairman, is a smoke. The meeting is finnee.

CULLEN Ah, good.

(*There is a general relaxation.* SHAWN *is muttering a few soft 'I do's' on the phone.* JOE HOOP *stands up, marches to the door, turns and gives a loud thick smiling 'Good night' and is gone.* CULLEN *starts putting on his coat and hat briskly.*)

CULLEN I'm afraid we'll have rain. My corns are telling me so.

SHAWN (*on phone, simultaneously with following conversation*) Ah, yes. I do, I do. The little ferim. It is indeed. A

rich . . . fertile . . . richly-cultivated . . . grand . . . fine . . .
delightful . . . little ferim. Ah, glory be to God, a grand . . .
rich . . . fertile . . . glorious . . . well-appointed . . . healthy
. . . herbaceous . . . delightful ferim of land . . . yes.

KELLY (*rising wearily*) And small harm it would do us,
Martin, the wheat is a bit backward.

CULLEN (*going out*) O true enough. Good night.

SEVERAL VOICES Good night, now!

SHAWN (*on phone*) Yes, boy. I do, I do. Lovely, thick,
nourishing grass, grand . . . green . . . fertile . . . sweet . . .
lovely grass, sure I've eaten some of it myself, it's food for
man and baste, boy.

KELLY (*producing his pipe and beginning to fill it*) Town
Clerk, we will have a word together in the morning about
(*he numbers them on his fingers*)—the coal fund—the grant
for Patrick Street—the scavenging contract. We must look
into these things. We must take our coats off. Too many
cooks here. You and I must get something done. We will
feel fresher tomorrow and please God we'll put our
shoulders to the wheel.

TOWN CLERK (*absorbed in his papers*) I'll be here all day.
Any time you like. (*He looks at his watch and is startled; he
rushes over to* SHAWN *and nudges him urgently.*) Gob,
look at this crow. Come on out o' that man. It's ten to ten!
IT'S TEN TO TEN, MAN! See you later, Chairman!
(*He grabs his hat and rushes out.* KELLY *thoughtfully
strikes a match and begins to kindle his pipe.* SHAWN
stands up still holding the telephone.)

SHAWN (*urgently*) Well, goodbye, now, avic, I'm called
away on hard . . . important . . . business. I'll see you on
Thursday, boy. Bye, bye, now.
(*He slams down phone, grabs his hat and rushes out with a
'Bye, bye, Chairman.'* KELLY *grunts in reply. When they
are all gone* THE STRANGER *comes down noiselessly and*

gives KELLY *a great start by appearing suddenly at his elbow and beginning to talk in a very eerie colourless voice.*)

THE STRANGER I congratulate you. There was no doubt that I would get the job but nevertheless I congratulate you. Before many moons are past you will be a T.D. and every other wish you have will be gratified.

KELLY (*a bit agitated*) Yes, quite. Quite. Good.

THE STRANGER I will supply money and votes and everything that is required. Your love for Mrs Crockett will prosper. And now that I am a rate collector, there will be no undue comment about my staying in the town. I now have *locus standi* in the neighbourhood.

KELLY Quite. And as rate collector you'll have charge of the register of electors. The rate collector idea was a smart one, if I may say so.

THE STRANGER Everything will prosper for you from this day forward. Have no fear.

KELLY Yes. Good, good. (*Pause. Kelly rises and backs towards door,* THE STRANGER *moving after him menacingly.*) If you stay there a moment, I'll get the Town Clerk back to fix you up formally and give you the lists. He's having a drink next door.

THE STRANGER Yes, that would be wise.

KELLY (*backing out*) I won't be a moment.

CURTAIN

Act II

(Six weeks have passed.
Scene is the living-room of MRS MARGARET CROCKETT'S
house. The room is comfortable and furnished with taste but
is being used as the headquarters of an election campaign
and is on that account disarranged. Pinned to the back wall
are two posters. One reads VOTE FOR KELLY
AND A NEW BROOM. *The other* NOT FOR
PARTY NOR PRIVILEGE BUT FOR COUN-
TRY AND PEOPLE—KELLY. *There is a door,*
left back, and another (to other parts of house), left front.
There is a window, back right corner. On a side table are
boxes of envelopes and stationery, a few brass musical
instruments and a megaphone. In a corner stands an enor-
mous furled tricolour. There is a fire at side, right. At
back is a large two-doored cupboard which, when opened
reveals shelves of delf, tea-things, etc. The latter must be
constructed so that the entire inside of it is hinged in a
manner that will permit the action detailed towards the
end of the play.
  A bell rings. HANNAH *bustles in left, makes a frenzied*

attempt to clear up the litter, and then exits right. She is heard talking to someone off stage and in a moment re-enters leading THE STRANGER, *who is dressed as before but seems in a somewhat genial mood. It is evident that* HANNAH *and he are on good terms from previous meetings.* THE STRANGER *looks over the election paraphernalia appreciatively.*)

THE STRANGER Well, it won't be long now, Hannah. It won't be long till we are rewarded for all our work. But we're going to win. Remember that. (*He gives her a playful slap.*) We're going to win! (*Puts brief-case on table.*)

HANNAH Do you know, you're getting worse.

THE STRANGER Perhaps I am, but it's the excitement of this election. Rate collecting is a bit dull. We'll have a great party the night the results come in.

HANNAH (*still trying to tidy up*) Well, you won't have it here because you know what herself thinks about drink. It was the drink killed her husband. You can bring a Mills bum and put it on the mantelpiece there, but God help you if you try bringing in a bottle of stout. Are you sure they're going to make a T.D. out of poor Mr Kelly?

THE STRANGER Of course we are. Everybody's going to vote for Kelly. Wait till you see. They had a great meeting the other night.

HANNAH What about that necklace you promised me?

THE STRANGER (*surprised*) What? The necklace? (*Recovering quickly.*) O, you needn't think I forgot about it. It's waiting for you under that cushion. (*Points to divan.*)

HANNAH (*not believing him but going to lift the cushion to make sure*) Where—here? O, glory be to God! Glory be to God! (*Flabbergasted, she holds up a glistening necklace.*)

THE STRANGER What did I tell you?

HANNAH O, thank you, sir. When did you put it there?

THE STRANGER (*brushing the thing aside*) Now, now, no
questions. Is her ladyship up yet?

HANNAH She is, or she should be. She had her breakfast in
bed an hour ago. (*She turns round on* THE STRANGER
accusingly.) And if she's not up before now it's not her
fault. She had another late night last night with your
friend Mr Kelly. I declare to God I don't know what hour
of the night or day he left because I went to bed. It's not
respectable, that class of thing. (*She pauses to reflect.*) It
wouldn't be so bad if they were married, of course. People
think nothing of rascality and carry-on if you are married.

THE STRANGER Now, Hannah, Mr Kelly left at a respectable hour and always does. I was expecting to see him here
this morning. I've some extracts from the electoral register
here to give him. He has a committee meeting here this
morning. (*He takes a letter from his pocket.*)

HANNAH There's nothing but meetings here. (*A bell rings.*)

THE STRANGER Ah, here he is now. That's a real T.D.'s ring.

HANNAH It's early in the morning he's comin' back then.
(*She hurries out, right.*) I don't believe he's five hours out of
this house, but sure it's no business of mine. (*She returns
almost at once excitedly bearing a telegram.*)

HANNAH It's a telegram for the missus! A telegram! (*She
pauses in the middle of the stage on her way off, left.*) God
between us and all harm, I wonder what's in it.

THE STRANGER Good news, my dear girl, good news! Don't
be always expecting the worst.

HANNAH (*going out left*) Well, thank God *I* never got a
telegram.

THE STRANGER (*regarding poster on wall*) 'NOR privilege'
—'NOR privilege'! That's wrong. That 'nor' should be
'or'. 'Or privilege' it should be.

(*He walks over to the poster and passes his hand over it.
Revealed to audience is the same poster but with OR*

instead of NOR. *This can be done by having the 'N' printed on a separate slip of paper, lightly fastened to the poster.*)

HANNAH (*re-entering excitedly*) No, no, you needn't ask me. Her ladyship keeps her good fortune and her hardship to herself. Wouldn't even open a letter and read it in front of me. Waits till she's alone.

THE STRANGER Well, I still think it is good news, Hannah. (*He looks at a watch which he takes from his waistcoat.*) I think I'd better go away and try to get some money out of the ratepayers, if it can be done at all. (*He picks up his brief-case.*)

HANNAH Well, we all have to do a bit of work some time.

THE STRANGER When Mr Kelly comes, Hannah, will you give him these lists and tell him I'll look in and see him tonight. Will you do that for me like a good girl?

HANNAH (*taking the letter*) He'll get it safe and sound. (*She puts it on the mantelpiece.*)

THE STRANGER Well, goodbye, Hannah. (*Exit.*)
(*Then* KELLY *walks in suddenly.* HANNAH *is tidying around hearth.*)

KELLY Good morning, Hannah. Is Mrs Crockett up yet?

HANNAH That man with the hat was here again this morning, Mr Kelly. He was looking for you and left a letter. You just missed him.

KELLY I met him at the door going out. I had a word with him in the porch. None of the others have arrived yet?

HANNAH No, sir. Here's the letter, sir.

KELLY Thanks. Thanks, Hannah.
(*He sits down wearily and opens the envelope mechanically, showing no interest in the contents.*)

KELLY Mrs Crockett isn't up yet?

HANNAH Yes, sir, she should be here any minute. She just got a telegram.

KELLY A telegram? Who from?

HANNAH I don't know, sir. She didn't say, sir.

KELLY I hope it isn't bad news.

HANNAH Oh, I'm sure it's good news, sir. We mustn't always be expecting the worst.

KELLY (*sighing*) True enough, Hannah. True enough.

(*There is a ring.* HANNAH *hurries out left to answer it.*)

HANNAH That'll be the other gentlemen, sir, for the meeting. The missus should be down any minute, I don't know under God what's keeping her.

KELLY Ah, yes.

(*He takes some documents out of the envelope and begins looking over them idly.* HANNAH *re-enters followed by* TOWN CLERK.)

TOWN CLERK The top of the morning to you, Chairman.

KELLY (*wearily*) Good morning, Town Clerk. Is Cullen or Kilshaughraun not with you?

TOWN CLERK No, Chairman, I left word for them to folly me here.

KELLY (*rousing himself to a brisker posture*) These lists I have here are very promising if Cullen has marked them right. Our enemy Cooper seems to be very weak, on this side of the country anyway. According to these lists, we have about four votes in every five. Now could that be right?

TOWN CLERK Yerrah, man dear, you'll have more than that before the dawn of polling day, sure our campaign is only gittin' steam up. We'll have to bate the lard out of that Protestant that's up against you.

KELLY Ah now, Town Clerk, where is poor old Christian charity? Have we forgotten that altogether in the heat of the campaign? Are the Protestants not Christians also?

TOWN CLERK Yerrah, that's all me eye for a yarn, you won't win any election with that class of talk.

HANNAH (*who is pretending to be working but who stops every now and then to listen to the talk*) I believe Cromwell was a Protestant.

TOWN CLERK He was, and a good one.

HANNAH And look at England that's full of Protestants.

TOWN CLERK Ah, that's a different thing. You'd be a damn fool to be anything but a Protestant in England. There's a place and a time for everything, girl. What would you expect to find in the say only fish. It comes natural to them in England to be Protestants. But it's a very unnatural thing in Ireland.

KELLY Some of my best friends are Protestants.

TOWN CLERK Hand me over those lists, Chairman, till I run me eye over them. With any more of this class of talk we'll lose our deposit.

(KELLY *hands them over with a wry smile.* TOWN CLERK *sits on corner of divan.*)

KELLY Well, indeed, it wouldn't be any harm if Shawn and Tom Cullen hurried up till we get down to our meeting.

TOWN CLERK (*reading lists*) And the lady of the house, by the same token. (*Pause.*)

KELLY (*rises and starts to pace room*) Haven't we two rallies on Sunday in Tobberglas after the last Mass and Knock-aree at two o'clock old time?

TOWN CLERK Yes, it's all arranged. We've a man from the Waterford Chamber of Commerce to say a few words—it looks well, you know, for an independent business candidate like yerself. An' we're having the Patrick Sarsfield Fife and Drum Band for the Knockaree rally—half of the divils in that place go back to bed after their dinners of a Sunday and we'll have the divil's work to get them up again for the meeting.

(HANNAH, *bored, finishes her show of working and goes out left.*)

KELLY (*meditatively*) Yes. Fair enough. I think I'll say a few words about the banks. And emigration, that is bidding fair to drain our land of its life blood and spelling ruin to the business life of the community. The flight from the land is another thing that must be arrested at no far distant day. Please God when I get as far as the Dail I will have a word in season to say on that subject to the powers that be. And of course the scandal of the Runny Drainage Scheme is another subject upon which I will make it my particular business to say a few well-chosen words. Other members may sing dumb if they choose. Other members may be gagged by the party Whip. The opportunist and the time-server may not worry about such things. But please God if I win the confidence of the people of this country—if they see fit to entrust *me* with the task of representing them in the national assembly—I will speak my mind freely and fearlessly.

TOWN CLERK (*putting down the papers he is studying and looking quizzically at* KELLY) Well, be Gob, if you'd only talk like that when you're above on the platform, you'd have de Valera standin' down from the Governmint to make room for you!

KELLY (*carried away by his own talk*) I'm telling you now, the country is in a very serious position. We must proceed with the utmost caution. Neither Right nor Left will save us but the middle of the road. Rash monetary or economic experiments will only lead us deeper into the mire. What the country requires most is informed and strong leadership and a truce to political wrangling, jobbery and jockeying for position. We have had enough of that—too much of it. Public departments must be ruthlessly pruned. Give me a free hand and I will save you a cool hundred thousand pounds in every one of them. I warrant you that if the people of this country see fit to send me to the Dail, there will be scandals in high places. I happen to know a thing or two. This is not the place or the time to mention certain matters. Suffice it to say that certain things are happening that should not happen. These things are known—to me at least. I can quote chapter and verse. I have it all at my finger-tips and in due time I will drag the whole unsavoury details into the inexorable light of day. No doubt they will seek to silence me with their gold. They will try to purchase my honour.

TOWN CLERK (*sotto voce, after listening in amazement*) I wish to God somebody would try to buy me.

KELLY (*bringing his fist again on the table*) Will they succeed? Will success crown their attempts to silence me? Will their gold once again carry the day and make me still another of their bought-and-paid-for minions? By God it won't! By God in Heaven it won't!

TOWN CLERK (*again sotto voce*) Be Gob, I'd sell me soul for half-a-crown!

KELLY (*shouting savagely*) I won't be bought by gentile or jewman! I won't be bought! I'm not for sale! Do you hear me, Town Clerk? I'm not for sale! I'M NOT FOR SALE!

TOWN CLERK (*lifting his head*) Yerrah, Chairman, I'm not tryin' to buy ye. Sure I didn't make a bid at all. (*There is a ring.*) I'm only tryin' to run me eye through these lists here. Be Gob, there's some very quare people goin' to vote for you if Cullen's marks mean anything. There's a Fianna Fail T.D. down here.

KELLY (*in a high, excited voice, still pacing and ignoring the* TOWN CLERK) I'm going to break through this thieves' kitchen ... this thieves' kitchen ... of gombeenery and corruption. I tell you I'm going to make a clean sweep of the whole lot of them, I'll drag them bag and baggage into the cold light of day. And I won't be stopped by Knight or

Mason. Mark that, Town Clerk. I WON'T BE STOPPED BY KNIGHT OR MASON!

(*There is another prolonged ring in the silence that follows this outburst.*)

TOWN CLERK Here's them two divils Kilshaughraun and Cullen, late and good-lookin' after wastin' half the mornin'. And yours, too, Chairman.

(HANNAH *appears, somewhat flustered, and hurries across the stage to exit, left back.* KELLY *stops pacing, passes a hand wearily across his brow and subsides again in his chair with a sigh.*)

KELLY Ah, Town Clerk, it's not an easy world. It's not an easy world. But please God we will do what we can for Ireland before we die. Please God we will be of some small service to the old land.

TOWN CLERK Sure I've been servin' Ireland hard since I was born. And what thanks have I got? Me fees for fairs and markets were disallowed be the Minister last year.

(*Immediately towards the end of this speech an entirely unexpected figure enters the room, followed by a gaping* HANNAH. *He is a slim, tall man of about forty, very well and carefully dressed. He wears glasses and a small, carefully-tended moustache. He carries himself with the complete and somewhat alien assurance of the gentleman whose training makes him at home in any situation. When he speaks, it is with a comically exaggerated haw-haw English accent. He strides into the room and evinces a very slight well-bred surprise at seeing the* TOWN CLERK *and* KELLY *seated so casually in somebody else's house. The* TOWN CLERK'S *attitude to the stranger is entirely non-committal but* KELLY *shows somewhat hostile surprise.* HANNAH *retreats to the door left, but does not leave the room, being prepared to die rather than miss whatever* surprise is forthcoming. *The newcomer puts hat, stick and gloves on table near door.*)

SHAW Ao. Good morning. Good morning.

TOWN CLERK Good morra, sir. That's a grand spring morning, thank God. (KELLY *rises and stares inquiringly.*)

SHAW O yes, indeed, really marvellous weather. First class, actually. I say, my dear, is Mrs Crockett about? Would you kindly let her know that Captain Shaw is here?

HANNAH (*gaping wider*) Yes, sir.

(*She is dismissed by his easy imperious manner and goes out left with great reluctance.* KELLY *continues to stare. The* TOWN CLERK *feels that his cuteness is challenged and is determined to find out who the stranger is and what is happening.*)

TOWN CLERK But yesterday wasn't much of a day. Divil a bit of good yesterday ever did the spring wheat.

SHAW (*blankly*) I beg your pardon?

TOWN CLERK (*taken somewhat aback*) The weather wasn't up to the mark yesterday, sir.

SHAW Nao, the weather in Ireland is rather a bad show. By the way, may I take the liberty of introducing myself? My name is Captain Shaw. I have just arrived from the other side. Had a very rough passage too, by Jove.

TOWN CLERK I see.

SHAW Bad show, you know, fearfully trying on the stomach. Frightful business if you don't happen to be a good sailor.

TOWN CLERK (*behind divan, rising and extending his hand*) I'm terribly glad to meet you, Captain Shaw. I won't worry you with me own name because I'm only the Town Clerk of this town——

SHAW Ao!

TOWN CLERK (*moving left towards fire*) And this gentleman, Captain, is de Chairman. De Chairman of de Council, Captain.

SHAW Ao. (*He bows in a formal courtly way.*) Terribly
  charmed to meet you, I am sure.
KELLY (*relaxing and perceiving an opportunity for further
  political ranting*) I am glad to know you, Captain, very
  glad to have the privilege of your acquaintance. It always
  gives me pleasure to welcome to Ireland one of our
  cousins from across the wave.
  (TOWN CLERK *stands at fire.*)
SHAW Ao, really?
KELLY I always feel that in every visitor from England we
  have a unique opportunity to propagate amity and good-
  will between the two islands, a chance to undo centuries of
  distrust and ill-feeling, a God-given opportunity to bring
  the simple and just claims of our land to the notice of the
  mighty nation that lives and has its being at the other side
  of the Irish Sea (*he advances*)—a chance, if I may make so
  bold as to say so, to show the English people, without
  malice or rancour, mark you, what they owe us before the
  sight of God and how they may pay it to us. In a word, how
  we may still be friends after seven dark centuries of
  oppression.
TOWN CLERK (*impatiently, feeling that* KELLY'S *address is
  unsuitable*) Yerrah, Chairman, that's another story. That's
  a different day's work altogether. (*He sits down at fire.*)
SHAW (*somewhat at sea*) Yes, quite right, quite right. Quite
  right. (*He sits down uneasily.*)
KELLY (*warming to his subject again*) And please, Captain,
  let there be no misunderstanding on this matter. Some
  people will tell you that I am anti-English——
SHAW Ao!
KELLY —that I cherish for the great English nation nothing
  but venom . . . and scorn . . . and contempt.
SHAW Ao?
KELLY What is my answer? My answer is that nothing

could be farther from the truth. It is a lie. For the land of England I cherish feelings of the warmest regard. For the people who dwell there, the love and respect that is due to their dignity as human beings, the admiration that is due to those who have worked hard and well in the pursuit of material, if not spiritual, happiness. But what shall I say of the class that is in power in that fair and fertile land?——

SHAW (*at sea*) Ao?

TOWN CLERK (*with mock enthusiasm*) Hear, hear! Hear, hear!

KELLY (*accepting this as genuine and waxing even more rhetorical*) What shall I say of those who are charged before God with the rule and government of the English nation, not to mention its dominions, dependencies, mandates and colonies beyond the seas? What shall I say of the corrupt, misguided, obtuse and venal time-servers, who have brought, through a travesty of justice and government, shame and dishonour on the British flag? With what scornful word or phrase shall I stigmatise at the bar of history the interventions of successive British Governments in the affairs of my own country—IRELAND, the lamp of civilisation at a time when Europe sat in darkness, cradle of the faith and home of martyrs. With what pitiless and inexorable terminology will I lash and lash again these debased minions who have presumed to tamper with our historic race, to drive millions of our kith and kin in coffin-ships across the seven seas to dwell in an alien clime with the naked savage, who have destroyed our industries and our crafts and our right to develop our national resources, who have not hesitated to violate the sacred tabernacle of our nation to steal therefrom, defile and destroy our melodious and kingly language—THE IRISH LANGUAGE—our sole badge of nationhood, our only historic link with the giants of our national past—

Niall of the Nine Hostages, who penetrated to the Alps in his efforts to spread the Gospel, King Cormac of Cashel, Confessor, Saint and lawgiver, heroic St Laurence O'Toole who is the Patron Saint of Ireland's greatest city, and Patrick Sarsfield, who rode by night to destroy, no matter at what risk to himself, the hated foreigner's powder-train at Ballyneety! With what appalling and frightening curse, Captain Shaw, will I invoke the righteous anger of the Almighty against these wicked men who live in gilded palaces in England, cradled in luxury and licentious extravagance, knowing nothing and caring nothing for either the English masses, the historic and indefeasible Irish nation, the naked negro in distant and distressed India or the New Zealand pigmy on his native shore? With what stern word will I invoke the righteous anger of Almighty God upon their heads, Captain Shaw?

TOWN CLERK Glory be to God!

SHAW (*very uneasy*) Really, old man, that's a bit strong, you know. After all, you know, there are some very nice chaps in London. I wish you would meet some of my friends there. Of course, Ireland got a very poor show at one time, there is no getting away from that, the country was mishandled from the start. No country in the world would be more loyal if they got a good show. The English and the Irish should get together, you know, old man, because they're nice people—damn nice people.

(*Pause.* KELLY *walks over and shakes the astonished* SHAW *by the hand.*)

KELLY And nobly said, Captain, I admire a man who will fight his corner. I respect a gallant foe. Please do not think that I am suggesting that all knavery, corruption and governmental incompetence is concentrated in the land of England. Alas, poor old Ireland has her own share of it too. In this country, too, Captain, we have the grossest abuses in high places. We have double-dealing, backstairs influence . . . cliques . . . (*he gestures*) . . . bad blood between brothers . . . corrupt and debased ruffians in every quarter working to sell the pass . . .

(*He breaks off.* MRS MARGARET CROCKETT *has just hurried in from left. She is a coarse, dowdy lady of about 35, somewhat stout and vulgarly dressed. She pauses as she enters, astounded at seeing* CAPTAIN SHAW. KELLY *stands silent, ignorant of what the position is.*)

MARGARET (*to* SHAW, *excitedly*) What, James? You!

(*She hurries over to shake hands. He rises with well-bred sang-froid and suddenly becomes somewhat stern.*)

SHAW Hullo, Margaret. How are you?

MARGARET Very well, James. How are you?

(KELLY *begins to come forward.*)

SHAW Quite fit, thank you, Margaret, quite fit. And you're looking in the pink yourself. I sent you a telegram. Did you not get it?

MARGARET I only got it this morning a short time ago. I thought you'd be on the seven train in the evening. I could have sent the car if I knew you were coming.

SHAW Ao.

MARGARET It's a great surprise to see you, James. I don't think we have seen each other since daddy's funeral and that's a long time ago.

SHAW I believe you're right, Margaret. And that is quite a time, isn't it? By the way—(*he pauses and glances round at* KELLY *and the* TOWN CLERK)—by the way, Margaret, I should like to talk to you about something very important.

MARGARET (*coming between* SHAW *and* KELLY) Yes. You know these gentlemen? They are friends of mine, very special friends—(*indicating* KELLY) this is the Chairman of the Urban Council in person. And this is his officer, the Town Clerk. (*She turns to* KELLY *and indicates* SHAW.)

This is my brother, Captain Shaw. (KELLY *and* TOWN CLERK *are astonished.*)

KELLY *Your brother!* I didn't know you had a brother, Margaret. You never told me.

TOWN CLERK Well, do you know, there's a family resemblance there all right.

MARGARET (*smiling*) Well, you know, out of sight, out of mind. I haven't seen James for nearly eighteen years. James lives in England and has lived there nearly all his life. And that's why it's such a shock to see him. (*She becomes anxious suddenly.*) There's nothing wrong, James, is there? (*Sits on divan.* KELLY, TOWN CLERK *and* SHAW *sit.*)

SHAW Ao, nao. I just dashed across to have a talk with you, Margaret. A heart to heart chat, you know, old girl.

KELLY Ah, yes. I see. I see.

TOWN CLERK Ah, sure the family tie is a grand thing.

SHAW Black show, all right, breaking up of the home and the scattering of the family and all that. D'you know, I feel quite a foreigner here. And yet I'm Irish, aren't I?

TOWN CLERK Yerrah, Captain, wait till you get a drop of the good ould crature into you. That'll make you feel Irish again, that and a good feed of Cork crubeens.

SHAW Ao, really?

KELLY (*rising, with an air of briskness*) Now, Town Clerk, this is no place for us. Family conferences as I understand them must be conducted in strict privacy. Any other person, intimate friend of the family though he be, must in no circumstances intrude or violate that intimate and sacred privacy. Captain Shaw, I hope and pray I will have the pleasure and the privilege of meeting you again before you depart from our midst. (SHAW *and* MARGARET *rise.*)

SHAW (*bowing*) A great pleasure, I am sure, old man.

TOWN CLERK Well, we'll skidaddle, me an' the Chairman. Let ye have ye'r talk here in peace. (*He moves to door, left.*)

MARGARET Well, it's a shame to be pushing you out like this but James doesn't come to see me every day.

SHAW Yes, you chaps, rather black show crowding you out, you know, but I want to talk to my sister here about a blighter called Kelly. The old girl hasn't been behaving very sensibly, I'm afraid. A very bad hat, I'm told.

TOWN CLERK (*astounded*) Well, glory be to God!

(KELLY *has stopped in his track at the door and turned round, gaping.*)

MARGARET *James!*

KELLY What?

MARGARET James! What are you saying? This is Mr Kelly.

(KELLY *steps back a few paces into the room.*)

MARGARET (*coming over excitedly between* KELLY *and* SHAW) James, what on earth do you mean? This is Mr Kelly.

KELLY *My* name is Kelly. (*He strikes his breast.*) I'm Kelly!

SHAW Ao, I say, look here——

MARGARET (*shrilly*) James, what nonsense is this you're talking? Mr Kelly is a friend of mine. Has some scandal-giver in this town been writing to you?

TOWN CLERK Begor, I wouldn't put it past Reilly.

SHAW (*stiffening*) Margaret, kindly stand aside. (*He approaches* KELLY, *gently pushing his sister out of the way.*) Do I take it that you are the same Kelly who is going forward as an Irish M.P.?

KELLY (*defiantly*) I have been persuaded by friends that it is my duty to offer them my services as their representative in Doll Erin.

SHAW Very good. Then we know each other, we know where we are. Allow me to tell you, sir, that you are a cad.

MARGARET (*distressed*) James!

SHAW (*ignoring her*) Do you hear me? A cad, a rotter and a bounder!

KELLY (*angrily*) How dare you talk to me like that! How dare you!

SHAW I have not finished with you, sir. I have called you a cad. I now call you an unspeakable cur.

KELLY (*shouting to* MARGARET *and striding past* SHAW *to the other side of the stage*) What the devil is all this about? How dare you use language like that to me! Margaret, what is wrong with this man?

SHAW (*facing sternly to* KELLY *again*) Kindly leave my sister out of this. You have damaged and destroyed her fair name enough already. If you were a younger man I should invite you to step outside. What your type of person wants is a damn good hiding——

TOWN CLERK (*coming forward uneasily*) Now for God's sake we don't want any fightin'. What we want is explanations. Explanations.

MARGARET (*retreating and collapsing in despair in armchair near fire*) O, my God!

KELLY (*in a hard, low voice*) You say that your name is Captain Shaw. Very good. I am trying to keep my temper. I demand—and at once—an explanation of your last calumnious and insulting utterance. Otherwise I will have to consider asking the Town Clerk to call a Guard. I will have you given in charge for criminal libel!

MARGARET (*moaning*) O dear, dear, dear.

SHAW I'll tell you very briefly what you are, you cad. My sister, Margaret, does not understand the world. You have destroyed her good name. You have spent whole nights in this house. You have given her the reputation of . . . a jezebel . . . a prostitute . . .

MARGARET (*her voice rising to a scream*) James!

SHAW (*continuing steadily*) You have given her the reputation of a prostitute in her own town, you low bounder. You have extracted money from her. You have made her

♣ 163 ♣

the tool of your greed for power and position and for that social standing—for that social position—which always seems so attractive to a low country public-house keeper. You have made her the tool of your vulgar and nauseating bid to become an Irish M.P.

KELLY (*very quietly, and turning away from* SHAW) I ask God to give me the grace to control my temper.

MARGARET (*rising up angrily and confronting her brother*) James, you ought to be thoroughly ashamed of yourself. How dare you talk about me like that? How dare you say I am an evil woman!

SHAW I said that this rotter has given you that name in this town.

KELLY (*exploding*) How dare you! How dare you!

MARGARET And what do you mean by walking into this room and making wild and base attacks on Mr Kelly, a gentleman you never saw before in your life? Who told you those lies?

KELLY What poisonous tongue or pen has been sowing discord and slander and calumny?

SHAW Have you spent nights in this house up to five and six in the morning? Have you received large sums of money from my sister? Did you cash a cheque of hers for forty pounds last Thursday to pay a printing bill?

TOWN CLERK Mrs Crockett is de Treasurer of de Election Committee. We put de election funds into de bank and den de Treasurer writes de cheques.

SHAW Who the devil are you?

TOWN CLERK (*sweetly*) A mimber of the gineral public.

MARGARET (*to* SHAW) You have disgraced me and yourself.

SHAW Now, old girl, you please keep out of this disgusting business. I am here because it is my duty to be here. I am your brother and I am the head of the family——

MARGARET You have never since I was born—since I was

born—done anything but meddle with me—and tell tales on me—and interfere with me. (*Her voice rises hysterically.*) You tried your best to have my own money bottled up with trustees, you tried——

SHAW Now, for heaven's sake don't make a scene. (*The door bell rings.*)

KELLY (*going over to console her*) Now, now, Margaret. Leave this to me. Everything will be all right. (*Leads her to armchair at fire.*)

SHAW You get away from that lady! Do you hear me, you cad!

(HANNAH *enters, stands flabbergasted for a moment, says* 'Glory be to God!' *and exits right to answer door.*)

KELLY (*fiercely*) I'll take no orders from you, you wretched English bully, you impudent pup.

TOWN CLERK (*to* SHAW) Now, Mr Shaw, as a bystander, I can tell you that you're making a holy show and a terrible exhibition of yourself.

SHAW Who the devil are you?

TOWN CLERK A mimber of de gineral public.

(*Voices are heard outside.* HANNAH *enters looking flustered and followed by* CULLEN, KILSHAUGHRAUN *and* REILLY. KILSHAUGHRAUN *with a thick* 'Bail o Dhia annso isteach!' *crosses the stage to an armchair left, throws himself heavily into it, crosses his legs comfortably, grins with good humour on the stormy scene, and sets about filling his pipe.* CULLEN *stops in surprise near the door.* REILLY, *who knows something and does not feel very safe, retreats to the background near the* TOWN CLERK *and endeavours to be as unobtrusive as possible.* HANNAH *crosses the stage as if to go off left, but in fact stands near the door listening. There is a few seconds' silence broken only by the sobbing of* MARGARET. SHAW *is surveying the newcomers with distaste.*)

CULLEN What's the matter? What's up?

KELLY You may well ask. You may well ask what's the matter.

SHAW (*to* CULLEN) Who are you?

TOWN CLERK (*sweetly*) He's a mimber of the gineral public.

SHAW This place is like a railway station. Margaret, what is the meaning of this? Have you no sense of shame?

KELLY Shut up, you bosthoon!

MARGARET (*hysterically*) How dare you speak to me like that! (*She struggles to her feet and faces* SHAW.) How dare you tell me what to do in my own house, and who to ask into it!

KELLY Hear, hear.

SHAW Don't be so damned theatrical, Margaret.

MARGARET But I know who to have in this house and who not to have. I know who to order out! Get out—you! Yes, you! You! Do you hear me? (*Her voice rises to a scream.*) Get out! Get out! (*She breaks down and rushes over to* HANNAH.) O, Hannah!

(*Pause.* HANNAH *takes her and leads her out left. There is a long awkward pause.*)

CULLEN What in the name of God is going on here?

TOWN CLERK We've all met with misfortune. A fair man has come to us from across the sea. With very bad news.

KELLY This whippersnapper, believe it or not, is a brother of Margaret's.

SHAW I haven't finished with you yet, Kelly. Impertinent language won't help you.

KELLY And I haven't finished with you. Indeed I haven't started yet. You will not be the first pup in this town that I put in his box.

SHAW (*looking at* KILSHAUGHRAUN, *who is puffing contentedly in the armchair*) I happen to be a brother of the lady who owns this house——

KELLY And who ordered you to clear out of it a moment ago.

SHAW I happen to be a brother of the householder. My name is Shaw. May I ask who *you* are?

SHAWN (*smiling genially*) Me, avic? (*He rises.*) Ah, isn't it a terrible thing to hear anybody in Ireland asking who Shawn Kilshaughraun is? Mr Shaw. (*He takes* SHAW *by the hand, catching the arm by the elbow at the same time with his other hand.*) Mr Shaw, you are shaking hands with Shawn Kilshaughraun, an humble . . . hard-working . . . good-hearted . . . mimber of the historic Irish nation.

SHAW (*taken aback and shaking his hand free*) Glad to meet you, I am sure.

TOWN CLERK ('*introducing*' CULLEN) This is another mimber of the gineral public like meself. (*He turns to* REILLY, *who is skulking in the background.*) And this is Mr Reilly.

SHAW Hullo, Reilly. What on earth brings you here?

REILLY (*coming forward defiantly*) I just dropped in to tell the Chairman that there's an inspector from the Department in the town. He's above in the hotel and he's down to smell out the ready-up about the rate collector or my name isn't Reilly.

TOWN CLERK Begob, Chairman, if there's an Inspictor in the town, my place is me office. (*He grabs his hat.*) My place is me office. I'll see yez all later. You too, Mr Bernard Shaw! (*He hurries out.*)

KELLY (*sneering*) Huh! I notice that you're already acquainted with this distinguished visitor. By God, I see it all now. I know now who my detractor and persecutor is.

CULLEN Won't somebody tell me what's going on in this house? What's the trouble, Mr Shaw?

KELLY The man's out of his mind, Tom.

SHAW This man Kelly, if you *must* know, is a low swine who has destroyed my sister's good name and robbed her.

CULLEN What?

KELLY You heard that, Tom?

CULLEN (*to* SHAW) You must be off your head, man.

KELLY You heard that, Tom? Make a good note of it. Mark it and note it well because your testimony on it will be required at another place and at another time.

CULLEN (*amazed, to* SHAW) But surely, man, you're not serious? Sure if the Chairman wants to court your sister, hasn't he every right to?

SHAW If you don't mind, I'll be the judge of any matter affecting the honour of my family and the right of my sister to regulate her own life. (*Sneering.*) And her bank balance, too.

CULLEN My God, you must be crazy!

KELLY Listen, Tom, pay no attention. The man glories in calumny and detraction. I ask you, Tom, to make a note of everything that is said here. Not forgetting the part played by our mutual friend, Mr Reilly.

CULLEN What has he been doing? What's this about, Martin?

REILLY (*coming forward and standing near* SHAW, *facing* KELLY) Do I have to ask leave from you to attend to me own private affairs? I don't give a snap of me fingers for you or any other twister. And you won't get away with your ready-up about the rate collector and don't think it.

KELLY (*throwing out his hands and turning his eyes to heaven*) Ah, this poor man, this poor misguided man!

SHAW Sanctimonious nonsense of that kind will avail you nothing. I'm going to smash you up in this town, you rotter!

CULLEN (*horrified, crossing the stage to the left, where* KELLY *and* SHAWN *are, leaving* SHAW *and* REILLY *together on right*) Listen, Shawn, can't we do something in the name of God about this? This is awful and a reflection on the whole lot of us.

SHAWN (*puffing happily*) I do, I do, I do. 'Tis reminiscent of me own stormy . . . hard . . . advinturous election days when Shawn Kilshaughraun stood out alone aginst the besht brains in the country. Sure, 'tis many a row the Chairman will have before he reaches the free Parliament of the Irish people.

SHAW (*to* SHAWN) Many a row after he reaches there? I'll see that he's kicked out at this election even if I have to go up against him myself.

REILLY (*astonished*) Go up yourself?

SHAW (*staring at* REILLY. *There is a pause.*) And perhaps it's not a bad idea at that. *Perhaps it's not a bad idea at that!* Why shouldn't I go up against him? WHY SHOULDN'T I?

REILLY Are you gone crazy, man?

CULLEN (*flabbergasted*) You go up? You a T.D.?

KELLY (*to* SHAWN) I told you the man wasn't right in the head. I told you.

SHAW (*pleased with himself, looking to each of them in turn*) Why shouldn't I go up? I'm Irish, aren't I? I'm Irish. I have the money. Why shouldn't I go up and expose and defeat this rotter on his own ground? What do you say, Mr Reilly?

REILLY (*puzzled*) Well, begob, Mr Shaw, I don't know what to say. I don't know what to say. (*He scratches his head in perplexity.*) Begob, maybe you wouldn't be the last man in the world to be appointed.

SHAW (*pleased*) D'you know, I think I will go up. I think I will go up.

SHAWN Begob now, three candidates would make it a grand . . . fine . . . heart-rending . . . pulsating election fight. (*He rubs his hands gleefully.*)

SHAW (*beginning to pace and think*) Yes. Quite. Quite . . .

REILLY Begob if you're not coddin' about going up you'll

have to look snappy. You haven't much time left. You'll have to get your committee goin' and get good substantial men to nominate you, and get posters printed. And all that takes money—bags of money. Could you put your hands in your pocket for a thousand pounds?

SHAW (*still thinking*) I have the funds, old boy, I have the funds.

SHAWN Yerrah, sure Mr Shaw has the stuff. I'd know that to take wan look at him.

KELLY Lord save us, the next thing you'll see me doing is laughing. LAUGHING! (*He gives a long forced hollow guffaw.*) The idea of it! The idea of it!

SHAWN Yerrah, boy, if he wants to go up isn't he entitled.

KELLY (*half to himself*) The idea of it! The idea! And something tells me that if this lunatic goes up, it certainly won't do me any harm. Listen, Shawn . . .

(*He goes over and begins to converse* sotto voce *with* SHAWN. *The only audible portion of the latter's replies is the phrase 'I do, I do'.*)

REILLY (*rubbing his hands*) Begob, do you know, Mr Shaw, I think you're the man we're all looking for. I think you'd be a good match for all the political rogues we have in this bloody country. I think you'd know how to down-face the bastards and clean up all this dirty jobbery and back-door stuff.

SHAW I'm Irish, anyhow—born within two miles of this town.

REILLY (*to* SHAW, *confidentially*) Listen here, Mr Shaw. You say you're Irish and that you come from this part of the country. Well, you speak like a man that spent a long time across the water. Tell me this. Maybe you changed your colours like a lot more when you were over there. The people here wouldn't like that at all. Are you an R.C. still or did you learn to dig with the wrong foot?

SHAW Don't be an ass, old man. I was born a Roman Catholic, and please God when I am called I will still be a Roman Catholic.

REILLY (*loudly and jubilantly*) Ah, well, that's all right. If you're an R.C., that's all right. That's grand. Grand.

CULLEN Are you seriously going up or is all this a joke?

REILLY Of course he's going up.

SHAW I haven't the pleasure of your acquaintance nor do I know your name, sir, but I may——

REILLY Cullen. His name is Cullen. Tom Cullen and he's not the worst.

SHAW Ao. Mr Cullen? (*Bowing.*) Glad to meet you, I am sure. I may tell you this much, Mr Cullen. I *am* going up for election. Even if I never took my seat and never attended a single meeting of the Irish House of Commons in Dublin, I would still be doing the people of this country a great service. Do you know why?

REILLY Why?

SHAW Because by presenting myself for election I would be saving them from that ruffian (*his voice rises and he points at* KELLY)—that impostor of a publican. No matter how it is done or what it costs me, I will save the people from that gentleman.

REILLY (*cynically*) Good man yourself. Well spoken!
   (KELLY *has begun to glare at* SHAW *angrily and now walks over to confront him.*)

SHAWN The blood is up. The election blood is up. I do, I do. (*Pause.*)

KELLY God in His mercy has so far given me the grace to keep my temper and I do not intend to lose it now. The golden virtue of control—control of self—is a thing I have always endeavoured to practise. I intend to persevere in that. I will not let a person of your type deflect me from that purpose. But this much I *will* say. This much I will permit myself. In a lifetime extending over a period close on fifty years I have never had the misfortune to encounter a person who is a greater pup, a greater bags, than yourself. You have the effrontery to talk of your sister's money. Not one penny of that have I ever touched. Not one penny of it could I ever bear to touch. WHAT YOU SAY IS A DAMNED LIE!

SHAW It is the truth, you rotter, and you know it!

KELLY But what is more important is *why* you are so interested in your sister's money. What is more important is why you are afraid your sister should get married.

SHAW (*sneering*) Really? Really?

KELLY (*fiercely*) PERHAPS THAT IS WHY YOU LET LOOSE ON ME IN THIS ROOM THE MOST VILE FLOOD OF CALUMNY ... AND SLANDER ... AND FOUL LANGUAGE IT HAS EVER BEEN MY SORE MISFORTUNE TO LISTEN TO!

(SHAW *glares at* KELLY, *then rushes over for his hat and stick and makes for the door, where he delivers a parting shot.*)

KELLY And that is about the size and shape of it and please contradict me if I am wrong, Mr Kilshaughraun.

SHAW (*at the door, after taking up hat, stick and gloves*) If it's the last thing I do in this world, I'll break you into little pieces, so help me—I'll run you out of this house and out of this country, you objectionable little pig of a publican. I'll destroy you, do you hear? And I'll make sure of one thing. You'll never be an Irish M.P. YOU'LL NEVER BE AN IRISH M.P. YOU——*

CURTAIN QUICKLY

* Insert appropriate local term of abuse.

Act III

(*Four weeks later.*
The scene is the same save that the room is in a far more advanced state of disorder with posters, stationery, banners, flags and all manner of electioneering paraphernalia. A clock shows that it is about nine in the evening. The curtains are drawn.

MARGARET *is sitting disconsolately alone on the sofa, which is facing the audience towards the left of the stage.* KELLY *is listening on the phone, bending over a small table towards the right. There is complete silence for a few seconds after the curtain goes up.*)

KELLY What? What?

(MARGARET *sighs and passes her hand wearily across her brow.*)

KELLY (*eagerly*) Yes. Yes, yes! Good, good. Excellent. Yes? (*He pauses to listen.*)

MARGARET What does he say?

KELLY (*holding up his hand to silence her*) Are you sure of that? WHAT? (*He listens.*) Good! Ring me up later. I SAID RING ME UP LATER! Goodbye!

(*He bangs down the phone and turns to* MARGARET, *gleefully rubbing his hands.*)

KELLY Margaret, Margaret, I'm nearly home and dried. I'm nearly home and dried! (*He flops down on the sofa beside her and takes her hand.*) I'm nearly home, Margaret.

MARGARET (*dejectedly*) That's good news.

KELLY (*trying to cheer her up*) O now listen, woman, CHEER UP! (*He takes her hand again and looks at her entreatingly.*) Are you not glad I'm winning? Come on, now! Are you? Honest?

MARGARET (*looking up*) I am, I am glad. But I'm worried. I was thinking about things. I was talking to Father Healy today.

KELLY (*impatiently*) Now for God's sake you're not going to start again about this business of being a nun? You're not going to be a nun and that's all about it. You're going to marry *me*. You're not going into any convent, Margaret. I WON'T HAVE IT!

MARGARET (*turning on him suspiciously*) I believe you have drink taken again today.

KELLY (*shocked*) Margaret! Me? How can you say a thing like that?

MARGARET Well you had drink taken last night, and so had that Town Clerk.

KELLY (*soothingly*) Listen, Margaret, you're a little bit unnerved by the worry of this election and I don't blame you. You know in your heart I never touch it, Margaret. Don't you believe me, Margaret?

MARGARET (*putting her hand wearily to her head*) O, I don't know. I'm very worried. God forgive me for quarrelling with James. He has made a fool of himself at the elections. And I'm to blame for that. I was talking to Father Healy about people with late vocations. I'm sorry I didn't do what I wanted to do years ago. I'm honestly thinking of

♣ 174 ♣

going away. Away from all this bitterness and fighting. Nearly everybody in the town was drunk when they were voting. Father Healy was telling me all about it. Drink, drink, drink.

KELLY Listen, Margaret, don't be talking like that. Public life is by no means perfect but please God we will change what is bad and shameful in it. And I said *we*, Margaret. You and I. Together we can strike a blow for the old land. Together we can do our small part to right the wrongs that have come down through seven centuries of alien domination and godless misrule. What do you say, Margaret?

MARGARET (*deflating him*) I can't get it out of my head that you take drink.

KELLY Margaret!

MARGARET Drink is what killed my husband.

KELLY (*earnestly*) I tell you, Margaret, I never touch it. I never touch it. (*He pauses and bursts out.*) My God, Margaret, why do you keep on saying that?

MARGARET (*sadly, in a preoccupied way*) Drink is what killed my husband. And my father. I would never marry a man that took drink. Never!

KELLY (*going over solicitously and sitting down beside her again*) Listen to me, now, Margaret. We won't go into the poor weak souls who were tortured and destroyed in the past by indulgence in bacchanalian vice. It is a branch of the national character which we must reform——

MARGARET And why must you go back to the past? Look at this town today. Look at that Town Clerk. He's the cheekiest little man in this town and he's always half drunk. He is always full of stout.

KELLY (*impatiently*) I know, Margaret, I know, but can we never talk of anything else? Listen, girl, I'm nearly certain to be elected. When I am and when I have taken my seat in the parliament of Ireland, can't the two of us get married and go up and live above in Dublin!

MARGARET (*still despondent*) O, I don't know what to say. But I don't know what I should do. I always wanted to enter religion. I don't like a lot of things I see in the world around me——

KELLY What things?

MARGARET O, a lot of things. Everything. I don't like the way people behave. It's not Christian. Look at the terrible things James, my own brother, said about you last Sunday. People are laughing at me—I know they are. I feel I am to blame for a lot of the trouble. And you are to blame too. We're all to blame. How could James say what he said on Sunday if he was a proper Christian?

KELLY (*indulgently*) Ah, Margaret, it's all poor old human nature. Poor sinful broken-down human nature. Bad as it is at the best of times, it goes to hell altogether when there's an election in the air.

MARGARET And how could you talk the way you did a moment ago about drink when you own a public-house yourself?

KELLY (*shocked and hurt*) Margaret, that isn't true. That isn't true at all. I don't own a public-house. It's only an off-licence.

MARGARET I don't care what it's called.

KELLY (*emphatically*) And it's only a six-day licence.

MARGARET Hannah was saying that she sees a lot of people going into your shop after the last Mass on Sunday, even though you're closed.

KELLY Ah, they would be the language workers—the Gaelic League. I give them a room free of charge for their classes, you know. I do what I can to encourage the old tongue.

MARGARET But surely people wouldn't be learning Irish at

that hour on a Sunday. I always though it's at night people learn Irish.

KELLY Yes, yes, Margaret, but there is such a thing as a committee meeting, there is such a thing as a committee of ways and means. The real spade work has to be done behind closed door. O, well I know it—many's a committee I served on.

MARGARET (*fiercely*) O, I don't care.

KELLY (*impatiently*) Listen, Margaret. (*He takes her hand ingratiatingly.*) One simple question now. The same one I asked before. Margaret, will you marry me? Yes or No? After I get my seat, of course. Will you marry me? Will you?

> (*The telephone rings violently.* KELLY, *startled, jumps up and without a word takes up the receiver; just when he has begun listening he remembers to say 'Excuse me' to* MARGARET, *who looks very disconcerted by his abrupt departure from her.*)

KELLY (*excitedly*) Hullo! Yes? Yes. What? (*There is a long pause.*) WHAT? Yes. YES. I AM? Are you certain? Good! Great! GREAT! Thanks, thanks, thanks.

> (*He bangs down the receiver and rushes exuberantly about the room, rubbing his hands gleefully; he is beside himself with delight.*)

KELLY I'm home, Margaret. I'm home and dried. The votes aren't all counted but he can't beat me now no matter what happens! Cooper's second and your brother's last! Master James is beaten, beaten to the ropes. HE'S BEATEN! And I'm in—I'm elected. I'm in!

MARGARET (*rising*) Are you sure?

KELLY Certain. CERTAIN! Sure I just got it on the wire.

> (*The front door bell rings.*)

MARGARET O, I don't know what to say to you! I'm glad.

> (*She rushes over to him impetuously; he catches her in a*

sort of half-embrace but this is broken almost instantly as
HANNAH *bustles in from left to answer the door bell. She*
exits left back, taking no notice of KELLY *and* MAR-
GARET. *Almost at once, the confused, thick babel of* SHAWN
KILSHAUGHRAUN *and the* TOWN CLERK *is heard from*
without. In a second they march in, SHAWN *leading the*
way. The TOWN CLERK *is three-quarters drunk but has long*
experience in disguising the fact. SHAWN *is not the type that*
can be changed by drink and for all anybody knows may be
completely drunk. His hand is already outstretched on the
way in preparation for a handclasp of congratulation.
MARGARET *has begun to retreat again from* KELLY *and*
sits down again on the sofa.)

KELLY (*beaming*) Well, well, well.

TOWN CLERK (*only half in through door*) Good evenin' one
and all. And good evenin' yourself, Mrs Crockett.

SHAWN Ah, Chairman, Chairman, may you long live to
wear the great, grand, fine honour that has been saddled on
you this day by the people of this grand old historic
country. May you live for long, long years to enjoy—and
re-enjoy—every bit of it—every little bitteen of it, avic.

TOWN CLERK (*coming forward to take* KELLY'S *hand away*
from SHAWN) Congratulations, Chairman. Begob you're
the right boyo. Sure I always knew you were a potential
T.D.—you were threatened with it since the cradle, man.

KELLY (*genially*) Thank you, gentlemen, thank you. Thank
you very much.

TOWN CLERK Yerrah, not at all.

KELLY This much I *will* say. Never has a public man been
the fortunate recipient of more whole-hearted co-operation
and assistance from true friends than I was on the occasion of this great election. (*He turns to* MARGARET.)
Margaret, I owe more than I can ever repay to these two
gentlemen——

SHAWN (*grinning broadly*) I do, I do.
  (*He makes his way heavily to the armchair near fire and sits.* KELLY *runs over again to* MARGARET *and sits down beside her solicitously.*)
KELLY Margaret, these are the two best friends I have. Both of us should be grateful to them, Ellen.
MARGARET Yes, I know. They worked very hard.
TOWN CLERK Yerrah now, don't be talkin' to me, shure it's only part of the day's work. 'Tisn't worth a fiddler's curse.
MARGARET And what about your other friend? The man that wears the bowler hat. The rate collector.
KELLY (*not so pleased*) O, him?
SHAWN I do, I do. Shure he worked like a steam-injun and he got hundreds of pounds from nowhere, wherever the devil he collected it.
KELLY Yes. He also showed himself a good friend.
TOWN CLERK (*sotto voce*) An' why wouldn't he, after been lurried into a job.
  (SHAWN *has genially lowered himself into a chair and begun the long operation of preparing his pipe. The* TOWN CLERK *wanders to a backward position where he is not visible to the two on the sofa, takes a half-pint from his hip pocket and takes an enormous slug.*)
SHAWN I do, I do. I congratulate you again, Chairman, but may the Lord comfort you and give you strength to bear the sad ... terrible ... mortifying ... excruciating ... fierce ... trials and tribulations that you will meet with above in the Dail. Shure 'tis like goin' to bed with ten crocodiles—and without your boots on you itself.
KELLY (*smiling*) Ah, well, please God we will try, Shawn——
  (*At this point the* TOWN CLERK *has taken his enormous slug of whiskey and gives an involuntary gasp or grunt that is clearly heard.*)
KELLY (*turning in surprise*) What——?

TOWN CLERK (*covering up hastily*) I was only clearin' me throat, Chairman. These cigarettes has me destroyed.

(MARGARET *wheels round and gets up, outraged by this noise. She moves back right, colossally irritated.* KELLY *shows concern.*)

KELLY What's the matter, Margaret?

MARGARET O, nothing. Nothing at all.

SHAWN Shure aren't we all worn away with the excitement of this wild . . . mad . . . ferocious . . . exciting day.

MARGARET (*testily, facing them all generally*) I think it's yourselves you're all thinking about all the time, not other people. You don't care what happens as long as you get your own way——

KELLY Margaret, what's the matter?

MARGARET It's true. You're like three peacocks here only that one of the peacocks has drink taken.

TOWN CLERK (*who has become a bit hilarious after the last slug*) That's a bit of a crack at you, Chairman.

KELLY (*very seriously*) Margaret, please——

MARGARET All the talk about Ireland and the fine promises we heard for the last month are forgotten now. And all the hard un-Christian things that were said—it doesn't matter about them, we're all very nice and happy and good-humoured now because we've won.

KELLY (*quietly*) Margaret, are you not being a little bit unfair? It is perhaps true that in politics there is much that is unpleasant. But speaking for myself (*his voice rises as he unconsciously climbs into his plane of ranting*) speaking for myself, this much I *will* say. As an accredited deputy in the national parliament I am determined to serve my country according to my lights and to the utmost of the talents which God has given me. I am determined to strike blow after blow against the vested interests. I am determined to break—to smash—backstairs jobbery in high places. I am determined to expose—to drag into the inexorable light of day—every knave, time-server, sycophant and party camp-follower. I will meet them all and fight them. I will declare war on the Masons and the Knights. I will challenge the cheat and the money-changer——

MARGARET (*in a loud, shrill, half-hysterical voice*) O, stop it. STOP IT! (*She begins to move restlessly about the room.*) I am sick—absolutely sick—of that sort of talk. I have listened to nothing else for a whole month. I simply won't stand any more of that. (*She turns on* KELLY *fiercely.*) Do you hear me, I won't stand it! (*She sits on divan.*)

SHAWN Yerrah shure we're all very tired.

KELLY (*going and sitting down beside her once again*) Listen, child, you're very tired. I think we should all leave you and let you get to bed.

(*The* TOWN CLERK, *getting the pair seated again, retires to the background, produces the bottle and takes an even greater slug than the previous one. He gives another loud gasp.* KELLY *turns and gives him a long cold stare, realises what has happened and looks back again to* MARGARET.)

SHAWN (*rising, with many affectionate pats and adjustments at his clothes*) I do, I do. 'Tis time and more than time for all those who have laboured for the grand cause to steal away (*he tones his thick voice down to a level that is meant to be dainty*) quietly into the sweetness of the night and to take a few sweet hours of soft salubrious sleep. What do you say, Town Clerk?

(KELLY *is talking inaudibly to* MARGARET. *At this point the door-bell rings. It is a most unusual ring—sustained for ten or fifteen seconds as if the ringer suddenly dropped asleep with his finger on the bell. Just as it stops* HANNAH *rushes in in great haste. As she exits right to answer the ring, the bell peals again and apparently is stopped only by the door being opened meanwhile.*)

TOWN CLERK Who in the name of God would this be now? Has he no shame to be calling to a private house at such an hour? Or would it be a Guard on duty?

MARGARET (*wearily*) O, I suppose it's more of these election people.

KELLY Well dear knows it is no supporter of mine and if it is he will march straight out again.

(*He is interrupted as* HANNAH *rushes in, very frightened and casting apprehensive glances behind her. In a second or two the reason for her alarm appears. It is* CAPTAIN SHAW. *He pauses absolutely still on the threshold. His clothes look somewhat bedraggled and his face bears an extraordinarily tense expression. All present are astonished and at the same time tense that something unusual has happened. They gape at* SHAW *and* MARGARET *rises to her feet in consternation.*)

MARGARET (*rising, as does* KELLY *also*) Jim! What's the matter? (*She takes a step forward.*) What's the matter, Jim?

KELLY It's our friend back again.

MARGARET (*her voice rising somewhat hysterically*) Jim! What's wrong with you?

TOWN CLERK (*who senses what is the matter from his own extensive experience and rushes forward to support* SHAW) Yerrah, sure the poor unfortunate man has been consolin' himself. And why wouldn't he!

(SHAW *is still standing wild-eyed at the door.* MARGARET *takes another step forward and stares at him as if unable to believe the suggestion made by the* TOWN CLERK.)

SHAWN (*softly*) I do, I do. He is happy in himself at last, God bless him.

MARGARET (*almost screaming*) Jim! Have you been drinking?

KELLY (*very quietly*) Sure the unfortunate man is stuffed with whiskey.

(*Here* SHAW *moves or falls forward into the room. He is in the last blithering stages of intoxication and the nature of his movements and attempts at talking is more a matter for playing rather than for writing in the present script; only the outline of his remarks is attempted here. He staggers over towards* SHAWN *and attempts to hold out his hand as if to confer congratulations.*)

MARGARET (*beside herself*) *Jim!*

SHAW No hard feelings, old boy.

SHAWN (*genially*) Ah, yerrah, the poor man!

SHAW No hard feelings, old boy. No hard feelings.

MARGARET (*rushing over and confronting* SHAW) Jim, you've been drinking! You've been drinking! *You*, that never touched drink in your life!

SHAW H'llo, Margaret. (*He peers at* SHAWN.) You're not Mr Kelly.

KELLY *I'm* Kelly.

TOWN CLERK (*almost simultaneously*) This is the elected representative of the people, Mr Kelly, T.D.

SHAW (*blinking round vaguely*) No hard feelings, old boy. (*He distinguishes* KELLY *and turns round to him.*) I'm a sportsman. Always believe in shaking hands with the man that licks me. (*He tries to hold out his hand.*) Besht man won, old boy. No hard feelings at all.

(*He falls on divan.* TOWN CLERK *and* SHAWN *sit beside him.*)

KELLY This unfortunate man ought to be in bed because damn the other place he's fit to be in——

(*At this point* MARGARET *becomes really hysterical. The sight of her brother in this condition brings all her loathing for drink to a terrific climax. She rounds on* KELLY.)

MARGARET Look what you've done now! Look what you've done now! (*Then she looks in turn to* SHAWN *and the* TOWN CLERK.) Do you see the result of your handiwork? (*She points at* SHAW.) Look at him! Look at him. I hope you're satisfied. That's all I have to say. I hope you're satisfied.

KELLY Margaret for heaven's sake don't be talking like that!

MARGARET Why wouldn't I talk like that? You're worse than any of them. You're responsible for this.

KELLY *Me?*

MARGARET You! It's you that drove my brother to do this —to put himself on the same level as a brute beast—a man that lived for 45 years in this world without knowing what the taste of drink was. (*Her voice rises even higher.*) You're to blame for this. Do you hear me? You're the cause of it and you'll have to answer for it before God.

KELLY *I'm* to blame? How in the name of heaven am I to blame?

SHAW Let's all be friends.

MARGARET He's beside himself with drink. He must have been at it for hours.

KELLY How can you say that I'm to blame if a grown man chooses to make a beast of himself?

SHAW We're all sportsmen here. All good sports.

MARGARET It's you . . . and this wretched election . . . and all these lies and slanders. The whole lot of you are to blame, and me too. Do you hear that? Including *me.*

TOWN CLERK Yerrah, not at all.

KELLY You poor girl, you're overwrought. (*He puts his hand on her arm but she shakes it off.*) You're not yourself, Margaret.

MARGARET Leave me alone!

SHAW Do you know, old boy, I was never in better form.

MARGARET (*pointing at* SHAW) Just look at him. Babbling like a child, bereft of every vestige of his God-given senses. O my God this is terrible!

TOWN CLERK Yerrah, sure the man is only jarred.

KELLY Margaret, we'll go home.

MARGARET I'm finished with you all—for ever. FOR EVER, do you hear me? You talk about Christian charity . . . and decency . . . and reforming all the nasty things one sees today in this country. What are you, the whole lot of you, but vulgar despicable hypocrites, a gang of drunken louts, worrying all day and all night about your own delicate hides! I'm sick of you . . . absolutely sick . . . (*Exit.*)

SHAWN (*with great compassion*) Ah, the poor overworked . . . tired . . . good . . . religious-minded girl. (*He looks towards* SHAW.) And the poor . . . tired . . . worn-out . . . exstotiated brother.

(THE STRANGER *has entered unobserved.*)

KELLY (*pathetically broken, going to window*) Ah, dear help us. Dear save us and help us. She's going to leave me.

TOWN CLERK She is, faith. (*He notices* THE STRANGER *and turns to him.*) Begob, yourself with your hat on! Where the divil did you drop from? (*They all turn in surprise to see* THE STRANGER.)

THE STRANGER Good night, gentlemen. (*He advances towards* KELLY.) And congratulations to you, Mr Kelly.

(*He takes* KELLY *affectionately by the arm, and walks him away from the others, talking to him in an undertone. He pauses on one occasion to point to the prostrate form of* SHAW. KELLY *looks disturbed and frightened. He makes a few half-hearted efforts to shake off the linking arm, and replies in undertones. Meanwhile . . .*)

SHAWN (*giving the vastest and noisiest yawn ever yet attempted by a human being*) Well, do you know, nivver in his life was Shawn Kilshaughraun so exhausted and worn out . . . and emaciated with exertions . . . and strenualities.

TOWN CLERK Yerrah, don't be talking to me.

(*At this point* KELLY *savagely wrenches his arm free from*

THE STRANGER *and backs away from him and speaks in a loud frightened tone.*)

KELLY I will not, I will not! I'm not a T.D. I haven't taken the oath or taken my seat yet. That's not the bargain!

THE STRANGER (*soothingly, ingratiatingly*) Of course, of course, Mr Kelly. That's quite all right. There is no hurry at all. (*He turns to the others.*) A little private matter we were discussing. It will be quite time enough at the next session, in two months' time.

TOWN CLERK (*to* THE STRANGER, *severely*) Have you no sense of fitness, man, to be talking business to the Chairman in the hour of his triumph. Shure if you'd any sense, you'd be out swallying balls of malt like the rest of us.

THE STRANGER I am sorry if I intrude. (*He sits beside* SHAW *on divan. The bell rings.*)

KELLY (*still very agitated*) Town Clerk, private word in your ear. (*To the others.*) Excuse me.

(TOWN CLERK *crosses to* KELLY *at window. They whisper briefly as* SHAWN *says:*)

SHAWN Do you know, rate collector, we owe the half of our glorious triumph to your good self.

(*The door bell has rung and* HANNAH *hurries in to answer it. She pauses in surprise when she sees those present.*)

HANNAH Glory be to God, are yez still here! Yez have the mistress in a right state upstairs, whatever yez were doing to her. (*She hurries out right.*)

THE STRANGER (*to* SHAWN) Well, I think we all did our best. You did a fine day's work yourself, Mr Kilshaughraun.

SHAWN (*deprecatingly*) Ah, yerrah, no.

(HANNAH *returns, leading the way disdainfully for* REILLY; *she goes out immediately to left, after giving all a contemptuous look and giving a long stare at the prostrate form of* SHAW *on the sofa.* KELLY *has now separated from* TOWN CLERK. REILLY *has a satisfied sneer on his face.*)

REILLY (*gloatingly*) Good night one and all. I have just had a nice bit of news.

TOWN CLERK Begob it must be very bad news if you have it.

REILLY O, it's nothing much. Only that the Town Clerk got a letter from the Minister this morning. (*His tone hardens.*) The ready-up is knocked on the head. The wangle won't work. Do you know why?

TOWN CLERK (*surprised and serious*) How the divil do you know what's in the private letters I get in me office?

REILLY (*triumphantly*) Do you know why? Because our friend there (*jerking his thumb at* THE STRANGER) won't be sanctioned. HE WON'T BE SANCTIONED!

KELLY (*almost brightly*) If the appointment is not in order for one reason or another, Mr Reilly, I am as anxious as anybody that it should be terminated.

TOWN CLERK Begob to tell the truth it's an appointment I was nivver happy about.

SHAWN (*coming forward*) Well, do you know, I guessed this would come to pass because the Department is one of the most . . . complicated . . . yokes in the whole . . . civilised world.

REILLY There's goin' to be a right row, maybe a sworn inquiry. Just wait and see.

KELLY (*sharply*) You can spare us all your bad tongue, Mr Reilly. Our Council was always honest and above-board but we can make mistakes like everybody else. I am as anxious as the next man to rectify any mistake that was made in the past.

REILLY There's goin' to be hell to pay over the query form. (*He nods towards* THE STRANGER.) Your man's replies to the queries was all lies. The Department's Inspector checked them. All lies from the word go. And very serious lies some of them were. The Guards are on the job now, I believe.

THE STRANGER (*getting up from the sofa and coming forward*) What's the trouble?

KELLY (*bravely*) I'm afraid *you're* the trouble.

THE STRANGER (*puzzled*) How do you mean?

REILLY (*almost losing his temper*) Begob you'll find out all about it very soon, me bucko. You were wheeled in on the ratepayers' backs by a bare-faced twist and by your own pack of dirty lies on the query form. YOU WON'T BE SANCTIONED. Do you hear that? You won't be sanctioned, and you might get a stretch in jail for yourself free of charge, into the bargain.

TOWN CLERK This ould crow is right. You won't be sanctioned.

THE STRANGER (*puzzled*) I don't desire to retain this post very long. Mr Kelly and I have an arrangement.

KELLY O, I'm afraid you're out of it even now. If you're turned down by the Department, that's the end of it. If the Council keeps you on, they leave themselves open to surcharge and perhaps a sworn inquiry. And that's a very serious matter.

THE STRANGER (*somewhat perturbed*) I don't see any reason why I cannot stay on for a little time until I get another job. I'm entitled to some notice. You can get me another job, Mr Kelly, can't you?

TOWN CLERK Another job? Are you crazy, man? Have you taken French leave of your wits and senses?

THE STRANGER (*perturbed*) I don't understand. What do you mean?

TOWN CLERK Yerrah, man, where were you brought up? Here you are in the position of a man that wasn't sanctioned by the Department. It'll be all over the town be tomorrow morning. Shure you might as well be dead, man.

SHAWN (*with most emphatic approval*) I do, I do. I do, I do.

THE STRANGER I don't understand. What of it if I'm not approved? I lose my job. All I want is another job.

TOWN CLERK (*turning in despair to the others*) Yerrah, shure the man is mad.

SHAWN (*indulgently, to* THE STRANGER) Do you know, 'tis a hard . . . fierce . . . unmerciful thing to say, but in this part of the country a man that was not sanctioned by the Department—well, do you know, he was better off in Van Diemen's Land. He was better off in some faraway quarter . . . like the republic of China . . .

TOWN CLERK I'll enlighten you, boy. You can be up for murder and welcome. You can take a hatchet and cut your wife into two pieces. People will say you're . . . an odd class of a man. But this business of not being sanctioned—oh, begob that's a different pair of sleeves. Wait and see, boy. Wait and see. As long as you live you'll rue the day.

KELLY (*gravely*) Oh, it's very bad. It's very difficult.

SHAWN. 'Tis like havin' insanity on the mother's side.

THE STRANGER (*agitated*) But I have to stay here for a while. I must have a job. I MUST HAVE A JOB. Surely you can fix me up for a few weeks, Mr Kelly? I can't be fired out like this without warning. It isn't fair.

> (*During this speech the* TOWN CLERK *has again retreated to the background, whipped out his bottle and drained it in one ferocious gulp. He advances again, looking very fortified. He then adopts a most solemn attitude and gestures with his finger.*)

REILLY (*who has been listening curiously, surprised by the trend of the conversation*) I don't know which of yez is the greatest twister, but bedad ye're all of the one mind now. Begor, it's changed times. (*He turns.*) And me own teetotal pal footless there on the sofa.

KELLY The appointment was perfectly in order until the Department said their say.

THE STRANGER (*very perturbed*) I don't see why everybody should be against me like this.

SHAWN I do, I do. 'Tis a very serious thing not to be sanctioned. 'Tis a very dark thing.

REILLY It's the worst thing that could happen to you in this life. (*To* THE STRANGER.) Listen, mister-me-friend. Aren't you in digs below in Connors?

THE STRANGER I am.

REILLY I know you are. Try going back there tonight. Just try it.

THE STRANGER What do you mean?

SHAWN Ah, glory be to God, you don't think big Mick Connors would let a man that wasn't sanctioned spend the night under his roof?

REILLY Not bloody likely.

SHAWN Shure no decent man would be such an omadaun.

KELLY (*with resignation*) I'm afraid you're in a hole, my friend. I wish I could help you but this situation is beyond me. I fear it is beyond my capacity. Some things I can do. Others—I cannot.

TOWN CLERK (*swaying and returning to the attack*) Listen, boy. Listen now, boy, till I relate a story to you. In a certain town where I was before this we had a man that wasn't sanctioned. Thanks be to God I only met this thing once before in my life. And do you know, I will never forget it. Never, so long as I live. Don't be talkin' to me.

SHAWN (*nodding heavily*) I do, I do. I know the case well. Shure 'tis part of the history of Ireland, man.

TOWN CLERK (*as if appalled by the recollection of it*) Ah, glory be to God, it was one of the saddest—one of the most heart-rending misfortunes that I ever knew. And I've seen a lot of terrible tings in me time. But this was—Ah, 'twas terrible. Terrible.

THE STRANGER But what have I done? I haven't done anything wrong.

REILLY Whatever lies was in the query form the Guards is in on it. Begob *you'll* rue the day you ever met honest Mr Kelly. Mark that, me bucko.

TOWN CLERK (*still absorbed in his sad recollection*) Do you know, at the present time in all Ireland I don't suppose you have more than ten unsanctioned men. God be good to the unfortunate poor divils. (*He turns in consternation to the others.*) I'D RATHER HAVE THE LEPROSY! Do you know that? I'd rather have the leprosy.

THE STRANGER (*more anxious than ever*) Look here, I don't like this sort of talk. What do you mean?

KELLY (*retreating to have a look at* SHAW) I can only tell you that you have my heart-felt sympathy in your misfortune.

THE STRANGER (*shrilly, getting really frightened*) What on earth do you mean? Will you please explain?

REILLY (*genially*) I'll tell you. Number One, no bed for you tonight. Number Two, no cigarettes or beer no matter where you ask for them. Number Three, no answer to any question no matter where you put it in this town. You're a man that wasn't sanctioned by the Department. You'll know what that means before you're much older or my name isn't Reilly.

SHAWN (*nodding*) I do, I do.

TOWN CLERK (*reminiscently*) This other unfortunate divil had a very misfortunate wind-up at the latter end. It was kept out of the *Examiner* but I remember it well. He opened himself up somewhere with a bit of a shaving-razor.

REILLY (*shrugging*) Damn the chance of this fly-be-night

opening his neck. Only decent people take their own lives. Many's a time I've felt like it meself.

THE STRANGER (*in a low voice*) And why did this man commit suicide?

TOWN CLERK Yerrah, shure the man couldn't get his fare to America and what else could he do?

SHAWN There was once an unsanctioned man in me own part of the country, years—ah, years and years ago. The same day the letter came from the Department, he was on his way across the great blue ocean. Where did the poor gawm go but Boston, a place that is full of the grand sea-divided exiles of our land. Well, do you know, the first hotel he walked into it was thrown in his face. The hall-porter, do you know, was from my part of the country too. And the poor unfortunate man was put out on the street again.

TOWN CLERK Shure I know that case. He had to fly off to Mexico and spend the rest of his days living with dagoes and all classes of wild men.

THE STRANGER (*bursting out with great nervousness*) But supposing I don't want a job? Supposing I have enough to live on for a while? Supposing I lived here very quietly and never went out and never spoke to anybody?

TOWN CLERK Live where, man?

THE STRANGER Where? . . . Anywhere. If they won't let me stay where I am . . . couldn't I live with Mr Kelly? Couldn't I, Mr Kelly? Just for a few months till you take your seat? What's wrong with that?

KELLY (*horrified*) O no thanks, that wouldn't do at all. Wouldn't do at all, at all.

THE STRANGER But WHY?

KELLY The clergy wouldn't have it in the first place.

SHAWN I do. Father Healy is very strict about unsanctioned men in the parish. He says it gives great scandal.

THE STRANGER (*now thoroughly upset*) THE CLERGY? What have they got to do with it? THE CLERGY?

REILLY If you're in this town tomorrow morning Father Healy will have a word to say to you. *He'll* pack you out quick enough.

THE STRANGER (*shrilly*) What? A priest?

KELLY If you try to stay here you'll have no life, man. Nobody will talk to you.

THE STRANGER (*forgetting himself in his anxiety*) But I HAVE to talk to people. That's my job. I have to talk to them, to persuade them, to make them do what I want—I mean, I like talking to people ... (*He breaks off in confusion.*)

TOWN CLERK You'll have to do your talking to the Mexicans, like the other fella. (*The telephone rings and* REILLY *darts over to answer it.*)

REILLY What? This is Reilly. Yes, he's here. (*He listens.*) I see. (*He puts down the receiver looking very surprised.*)

KELLY Who was that?

REILLY That was Guard Shanahan. He's on his way up to ask a lot of questions about that query form and he says there's going to be a Petition.

KELLY A Petition——?

REILLY Yes, a Petition. You're not a T.D. yet. There was some monkey-work. When the last two boxes of votes were opened they were full of ashes. (*He turns to the others.*) What do you think of that?

TOWN CLERK (*astonished*) Ashes? Well, begor ... that's extraordinary.

KELLY (*incredulously*) *A petition?* Ashes! Well, upon my word! Upon my word!

TOWN CLERK (*briskly to hide uneasiness*) Well, do oo now, if there's a Guard comin' up here with his note-book and pincil I tink I'll mosey off and have a nice bottle of stout for meself. Cheery-pip lads! (*Exit.*)

THE STRANGER (*now thoroughly scared*) I have nothing to hide, gentlemen. If the police wish to see me I am at their service. I'd better get my coat . . . I'll be back in a moment. (*He opens the press at back of stage, unnoticed by all save* KELLY. *Revealed are the rows of delf, etc. He quietly closes it behind him.*

REILLY (*exploding venomously as he gets ready to depart*) Well, I'm a happy man tonight. I've smashed to smithereens the lousiest twist, the dirtiest ready-up, that was ever tried on in this town. I have fixed the hash of that customer gone out, who ever the hell he is. And if I know anything (*to* KELLY) damn the T.D. you'll ever be (*sneering*) . . . Mr Chairman sir!
(*There is silence.* SHAWN *remains sprawled on his chair, delighted with himself.* KELLY *remains prostrate on his chair, his head bowed. Immediately the general gloom is punctured by a very abrupt and bad-tempered entrance on the part of* HANNAH.)

HANNAH Well, this is a nice house! Drunken thollabawns turning the place into a bear garden and herself upstairs with a nervous breakdown from the carry-on ye had between the lot of ye in this room!

SHAWN (*with great compassion*) Ah, the grand . . . fine . . . religious . . . soft-hearted woman. 'Tis off home I'll bring meself this minute and lave her to her prayers.

HANNAH (*belligerently*) Aw, we've had enough chat out of you.

SHAWN (*rising and waddling out*) I do, I do. Goodbye to yeh, Mr Chairman. I do, I do.

HANNAH (*to* KELLY) And I'm talkin' to you too. Yourself and your friend on the sofa. (KELLY *looks up uncomprehendingly*) I'm going to make a pot of good . . . strong . . . black coffee. That'll give yez all the power to walk again.

(She bustles over to the press into which THE STRANGER *disappeared. She throws it wide open, again showing the rows of delf. There is no trace of* THE STRANGER. *While taking out the cups she half turns her head and keeps on scolding.)*

Because walk out of this house is what the pair of ye is going to do, and in double quick time, too. The divil himself couldn't make more trouble than the pair of ye. *(Exit with coffee pots and cups.)*

*(*KELLY *is left alone with the inert* SHAW. *He mutters the word 'Petition' a few times and gradually seems to recover. Still muttering the word he rises unsteadily to his feet and takes a casual look at the press. His eyes are staring.)*

KELLY Ashes? . . . A Petition? . . . A Petition? *(He strides about feverishly.)* A Petition? *(He becomes defiant.)* To the devil with their petition! TO THE DEVIL WITH THEIR PETITION! Simply because I choose to make a few Christian principles the basis of my scheme of life, they hate me—they *loathe* me—they seek to fling me aside . . . TO RUN ME OUT OF PUBLIC LIFE! But they will not succeed—do you hear me?—THEY WILL NOT SUCCEED. I owe a debt to this old land that bore me. That debt I will repay. THAT DEBT I WILL REPAY. And no contemptible conspiracy, no insidious intrigue, no treachery or trickery shall stand between me and my rightful place in the free parliament of the sovereign Irish people. IN . . . THAT . . . NATION-AL . . . ASSEMBLY I will lift a *fearless and unfettered voice* to lash and castigate the knaves and worse than knaves who have sold out the old land on the altar of mammon, I will assail without mercy the gombeen men, the time-servers, the place-hunters *(he takes up his hat)* the fools and flunkeys and godless money-changers—I'll out-wit them all and destroy them, DESTROY THEM

FINALLY ...
(In a transport of oratory, he has left the room towards the end of the speech. Instantly the Devil has re-entered from the press, this time attired in the ceremonial robe of black used in the Prologue. He has a document in his hand. The light goes down until he is standing only in a green spotlight, a figure of great horror. His lips begin to move and immediately the voices of the other characters are heard. The voices can be those of the characters themselves but it will appear that THE STRANGER *is mimicking them with diabolical skill.)*

SHAWN Shure didn't he marry a grand big heifer of a woman. I do, I do. I do, I do.

KELLY I will speak my mind freely and fearlessly in the parliament of the Irish people—and without regard to political expediency, the dictates of vested interests, or the crack of the party Whip!

TOWN CLERK Come out and have a glawsheen, it's tin to tin.

KELLY I won't be bought—do you hear me?—I WON'T BE BOUGHT!

REILLY There's a dirty ready-up here and I'm not going to stand for it! I'M NOT GOING TO STAND FOR IT!

SHAWN The grand ... fine ... nice ... religious-minded woman. I do, I do.

KELLY *(shouting)* Just because I make a few simple Christian principles my rule of life, they hate me—THEY HATE ME!

SHAWN *(very softly)* I do, I do. I do, I do.

THE STRANGER *(in his own voice)* Not for any favour ... in heaven or earth or hell ... would I take that Kelly and the others with me to where I live, to be in their company for ever ... and ever ... and ever. Here's the contract, his signed bond. (*He shows the document and tears it up savagely.*) I WANT NOTHING MORE OF IRISH PUBLIC LIFE! (*Pause; he turns away, suddenly weary.*) I'm tired. I'm going home.

BLACK-OUT AND CURTAIN

A Bash in
the Tunnel

J AMES JOYCE was an artist. He has said so himself. His was a case of Ars gratia Artist. He declared that he would pursue his artistic mission even if the penalty was as long as eternity itself. This seems to be an affirmation of belief in Hell, therefore of belief in Heaven and God.

A better title of this piece might be: *Was Joyce Mad?* by Hamlet, Prince of Denmark. Yet there is a reason for the present title.

Some thinkers—all Irish, all Catholic, some unlay—have confessed to discerning a resemblance between Joyce and Satan. True, resemblances, there are. Both had other names, the one Stephen Dedalus, the other Lucifer; the latter name, meaning 'Maker of Light', was to attract later the ironical gloss 'Prince of Darkness'! Both started off very well under unfaultable teachers, both were very proud, both had a fall. But they differed on one big, critical issue. Satan never denied the existence of the Almighty; indeed he acknowledged it by challenging merely His primacy. Joyce said there was no God, proving this by uttering various blasphemies and obscenities and not being instantly struck dead.

A man once said to me that he hated blasphemy, but on purely rational grounds. If there is no God, he said, the thing is stupid and unnecessary. If there is, it's dangerous.

Anatole France says this better. He relates how, one morning, a notorious agnostic called on a friend who was a devout Catholic. The devout Catholic was drunk and began to pour forth appalling blasphemies. Pale and shocked, the agnostic rushed from the house. Later, a third party challenged him on this incident.

'You have been saying for years that there is no God. Why then should you be so frightened at somebody else insulting this God who doesn't exist?'

'I still say there is no God. But that fellow thinks there is. Suppose a thunderbolt was sent down to strike him dead. How did I know I wouldn't get killed as well? Wasn't I standing beside him?'

Another blasphemy, perhaps—doubting the Almighty's aim. Yet it is still true that all true blasphemers must be believers.

What is the position of the artist in Ireland?

Just after the editors had asked me to try to assemble material for this issue of *Envoy*, I went into the Scotch House in Dublin to drink a bottle of stout and do some solitary thinking. Before any considerable thought had formed itself, a man—then a complete stranger—came, accompanied by his drink, and stood beside me: addressing me by name, he said he was surprised to see a man like myself drinking in a pub.

My pub radar screen showed up the word 'TOUCHER'. I was instantly on my guard.

'And where do you think I should drink?' I asked. 'Pay fancy prices in a hotel?'

'Ah, no,' he said, 'I didn't mean that. But any time I feel like a good bash myself, I have it in the cars. What will you have?'

I said I would have a large one, knowing that his mysterious reply would entail lengthy elucidation.

'I needn't tell you that that crowd is a crowd of bastards,' was his prefatory exegesis.

Then he told me all. At one time his father had a pub and grocery business, situated near a large Dublin railway terminus. Every year the railway company invited tenders for the provisioning of its dining cars, and every year the father got the contract. (The narrator said he thought this was due to the territorial proximity of the house, with diminished handling and cartage charges.)

The dining cars (hereinafter known as 'the cars'), were customarily parked in remote sidings. It was the father's job to load them from time to time with costly victuals—eggs, rashers, cold turkey and whiskey. These cars, bulging in their lonely sidings, with such fabulous fare, had special locks. The father had the key, and nobody else in the world had authority to open the doors until the car was part of a train. But my informant had made it his business, he told me, to have a key, too.

'At that time,' he told me, 'I had a bash once a week in the cars.'

One must here record two peculiarities of Irish railway practice. The first is a chronic inability to 'make up' trains in advance, i.e., to estimate expected passenger traffic accurately. Week after week a long-distance train is scheduled to be five passenger coaches and a car. Perpetually, an extra 150 passengers arrive on the departure platform unexpectedly. This means that the car must be detached, a passenger coach substituted, and the train dispatched foodless and drinkless on its way.

The second peculiarity—not exclusively Irish—is the inability of personnel in charge of shunting engines to leave coaches, parked in far sidings, alone. At all costs they must be shifted.

That was the situation as my friend in the Scotch House described it. The loaded dining cars never went anywhere, in the long-distance sense. He approved of that. But they were subject to endless enshuntment. That, he said, was a bloody scandal and a waste of the taxpayers' money.

When the urge for a 'bash' came upon him his routine was simple. Using his secret key, he secretly got into a parked and laden car very early in the morning, penetrated to the pantry, grabbed a jug of water, a glass and a bottle of whiskey and, with this assortment of material and utensil, locked himself in the lavatory.

Reflect on that locking. So far as the whole world was concerned, the car was utterly empty. It was locked with special, unprecedented locks. Yet this man locked himself securely within those locks.

Came the dawn—and the shunters. They espied, as doth the greyhound the hare, the lonely dining car, mute, immobile, deserted. So they couple it up and drag it to another siding at Liffey Junction. It is there for five hours but it is discovered (by 'that crowd of bastards', i.e. other shunters) and towed over to the yards behind Westland Row Station.

Many hours later it is shunted on to the tail of the Wexford Express but later angrily detached owing to the unexpected arrival of extra passengers.

'And are you sitting in the lavatory drinking whiskey all the time?' I asked.

'Certainly I am,' he answered. 'What the hell do you think lavatories in trains is for? And with the knees of me trousers

🍀 204 🍀

wet with me own whiskey from the jerks of them shunter bastards!'

His resentment was enormous. Be it noted that the whiskey was not in fact his own whiskey, that he was that oddity, an unauthorised person.

'How long does a bash in the cars last?' I asked him.

'Ah, that depends on a lot of things,' he said. 'As you know, I never carry a watch.' (Exhibits cuffless, hairy wrist in proof.) 'Did I ever tell you about the time I had a bash in the tunnel?'

He has not—for the good reason that I had never met him before.

'I seen meself,' he said, 'once upon a time on a three-day bash. The bastards took me out of Liffey Junction down to Hazelhatch. Another crowd shifted me into Harcourt Street yards. I was having a good bash at this time, but I always try to see, for the good of me health, that a bash doesn't last more than a day and a night. I know it's night outside when it's dark. If it's bright, it's day. Do you follow me?'

'I think I do.'

'Well, I was about on the third bottle when this other shunter crowd come along—it was dark, about eight in the evening—and nothing would do them only bring me into the Liffey Tunnel under the Phoenix Park *and park me there*. As you know I never use a watch. If it's bright, it's day. If it's dark, it's night. Here was meself parked in the tunnel opening bottle after bottle in the dark, thinking the night was a very long one, stuck there, in the tunnel. I was three-quarters way into the jigs when they pulled me out of the tunnel into Kingsbridge. I was in bed for a week. Did you ever in your life hear of a greater crowd of bastards?'

'Never,'

'That was the first and last time I ever had a bash in the tunnel.'

Funny? But surely there you have the Irish artist? Sitting fully dressed, innerly locked in the toilet of a locked coach where he has no right to be, resentfully drinking somebody else's whiskey, being whisked hither and thither by anonymous shunters, keeping fastidiously the while on the outer face of his door the simple word, ENGAGED?

I think the image fits Joyce: but particularly in his manifestation of a most Irish characteristic—the transgressor's resentment with the nongressor.

A friend of mine found himself next door at dinner to a well-known savant who appears in *Ulysses*. (He shall be nameless, for he still lives.) My friend, making dutiful conversation, made mention of Joyce. The savant said that Ireland was under a deep obligation to the author of Joyce's *Irish Names of Places*. My friend lengthily explained that his reference had been to a different Joyce. The savant did not quite understand, but ultimately confessed that he had heard certain rumours about the other man. It seemed that he had written some dirty books, published in Paris.

'But you are a character in one of them,' my friend incautiously remarked.

The next two hours, to the neglect of wine and cigars, were occupied with a heated statement by the savant that he was by no means a character in fiction, he was a man, furthermore he was alive and he had published books of his own.

'How can I be a character in fiction,' he demanded, 'if I am here talking to you?'

That incident may be funny, too, but its curiosity is this: Joyce spent a lifetime establishing himself as a character in fiction. Joyce created, in narcissus fascination, the ageless Stephen. Beginning with importing real characters into his books, he achieves the magnificent inversion of making them legendary and fictional. It is quite preposterous. Thousands of people believe that there once lived a man named Sherlock Holmes.

Joyce went further than Satan in rebellion.

Two characters who confess themselves based on Aquinas: Joyce and Maritain.

In *Finnegans Wake*, Joyce appears to favour the Vico theory of inevitable human and recurring evolution—theocracy: aristocracy: democracy: chaos.

'A.E.' referred to the chaos of Joyce's mind.

That was wrong, for Joyce's mind was indeed very orderly. In composition he used coloured pencils to keep himself right. All his works, not excluding *Finnegans Wake*, have a rigid classic pattern. His personal moral and family behaviours were impossible. He seems to have deserved equally with George Moore the sneer about the latter—he never kissed, but told.

What was really abnormal about Joyce? At Clongowes he had his dose of Jesuit casuistry. Why did he substitute his home-made chaosistry?

It seems to me that Joyce emerges, through curtains of salacity and blasphemy, as a truly fear-shaken Irish Catholic, rebelling not so much against the Church but against its near-schism Irish eccentricities, its pretence that there is only one Commandment, the vulgarity of its edifices, the shallowness and stupidity of many of its ministers. His revolt, noble in itself, carried him away. He could not see the tree for the woods. But I think he meant well. We all do, anyway.

What is *Finnegans Wake*? A treatise on the incommunicable night-mind? Or merely an example of silence, and punning?

I doubt whether the contents of this issue will get many of us any forrarder.

A certain commentator seeks to establish that Joyce was at heart an Irish dawn-bursting romantic, an admirer of de Valera, and one who dearly wished to be recalled to Dublin as an ageing man to be crowned with a D.Litt. from the National and priest-haunted University. This is at least possible, if only because its explains the preposterous 'esthetic' affectations of his youth, which included the necessity for being rude to his dying mother. The theme here is that a heart of gold was beating under the artificial waistcoat. Amen.

The number of people invited to contribute to this issue has necessarily been limited. Yet it is curious that none makes mention of Joyce's superber quality: his capacity for humour. Humour, the handmaid of sorrow and fear creeps out endlessly in all Joyce's works. He uses the thing, in the same way as Shakespeare does but less formally, to attenuate the fear of those who have belief and who genuinely think that they will be in hell or in heaven shortly, and possibly very shortly. With laughs he palliates the sense of doom that is the heritage of the Irish Catholic. True humour needs this background urgency: Rabelais is funny, but his stuff cloys. His stuff lacks tragedy.

Perhaps the true fascination of Joyce lies in his secretiveness, his ambiguity (his polyguity, perhaps?), his leg-pulling, his dishonesties, his technical skill, his attraction for Americans. His works are a garden in which some of us may play. This issue of *Envoy* claims to be merely a small bit of that garden.

But at the end, Joyce will still be in his tunnel, unabashed.